Also by Rosalind W. Johnson

Fiction

Friends To Die For
Secret Lives

Nonfiction

Roz' Little Manual For Surviving Potholes

T.J. Sloane

Rosalind W. Johnson

authorHOUSE®

AuthorHouse™
1663 Liberty Drive
Bloomington, IN 47403
www.authorhouse.com
Phone: 833-262-8899

Cover art by Wendy G Photography www.WendyG.com

Published by AuthorHouse 03/11/2021

ISBN: 978-1-6655-1515-3 (sc)
ISBN: 978-1-6655-1514-6 (e)

Print information available on the last page.

This book is printed on acid-free paper.

I am deeply grateful to my late son, James K. Johnson III and his father, James K. Johnson, Jr., for their encouragement in my literary endeavors. T.J. Sloane's story could not be told without my son's stated understanding of what can happen when race and culture intersect in today's world. It does not always result in the expected.

Every man's life is a storybook of many chapters. Each one filled with the drama of conflict, hidden fears sheltered by quiet dreams and love as it suits him. T.J.'s tale begins with the backstory of change and sudden loss. But this part of the narrative need not bind his hopes and dreams. On the other hand, ancient fears of violence challenge his self-determination with unreliable memories and sometimes, myth. Like a river rushing to the sea, his backstory is always chasing the present. If he ignores this segment of his journey, he does so at his peril.

1

How was I to know, as I stepped into the waiting car, in two hours my life would change forever? Nothing unusual about the cold December morning alerted me to the looming disruption I was about to face. The weather was typical; sharp wind gusts blew with steady force, foretelling rough months to come. Mr. Joseph, as was his habit, drove cautiously through heavy downtown traffic and I'd finally cleared my calendar for an extended holiday visit with my son. Unlike the previous morning, on that day my only concern was the team's readiness for our prolonged Shanghai negotiations.

When I arrived in my office, I immediately noticed a small pile of mail stacked on the conference table. On top was an unopened envelope with a familiar Mississippi State return address. I set it aside to read after attending to the regular morning mail. An hour later when I opened the envelope and began reading the enclosed letter, a morning that started as an ordinary business day, became instead, the day my world imploded.

> Mr. Sloane:
>
> You're receiving this notice because our records list you as next of kin. On Thursday, December 16th,

> Inmate No. 16590, Billy Cady, died peacefully in his sleep. His body has been moved to the county morgue. It must be claimed within thirty days. If not, it will be disposed of according to state regulations. Please let us know your intentions immediately. In addition to the body, all personal effects are available for pick-up. If you need assistance, contact the Department of Corrections, Office of Inmate Services at the address or telephone number shown below.

Stunned, cold numbness seized my heart, my mind rejecting the words staring back at me. I couldn't believe them. Forcing myself, I reread the message twice, concentrating on each word. But my mind played a reel of long-ago pictures of two young boys, always together. They were vivid scenes of happy times playing along rutted roads or sitting at the base of the old levee having serious discussions about our next day's activities. Even occurrences I thought were forgotten resurfaced. The last scene that looped around again and again, was of a man behind bars and bullet-proof glass, caged like a trapped animal with no way of escape. He would be remembered by few, other than myself. Billy's years of a life going only in circles, finally left him defeated. He gave up the fight to make his life relevant. I hope he didn't suffer.

Forty years of my life ended by a one-paragraph note without even the dignity of a signature. Despite the searing pain of loss, I immediately made arrangements for his body to be transported to Jackson. During the coming hours a sadness I'd never felt before engulfed me. By nightfall I was on a plane, my mind a jumble of churning thoughts. One after another, the memories still flooding my senses did nothing to ease my loss.

All the conflicts of your life have ended Billy. Thanks for everything. Rest in peace. Even though I will never know why you betrayed me, we are brothers still.

Almost a year has passed since Billy's death. His loss upended the settled existence I've spent a lifetime creating. Entrenched memories of the path that wove our lives together surface daily. They come to me as I need them to ward off creeping doubts about the authenticity of our friendship. My recurring focus, most often, settles on the last year of his life and our wide-ranging conversations during my visits. Even unbidden thoughts of my mother surface and she's been dead for more than twenty years. My memories of her are always interwoven with the contradictory emotions around an intriguing woman who recently entered my life. As these emotional conflicts become more pronounced, I must look back to the beginning, to Sero; the town that brought Billy and I together.

Some people call it luck. Others say I'm blessed. It is true I had a chancy start in life. My options improved, however, when I landed in a place, at a time, in the care of a woman who had an intimate relationship with luck and his close relative, chance. "Luck will lift your dreams," Grandma Neetha would say. "Chance is indifferent to them." How she was able to fine-tune the difference between these road signs, as she called them, I never understood. But one of these possibilities was the reason I started my life with her.

It was, however, pure luck when I met Billy and we began our lifelong friendship.

After the passage of so many years, at odd times, I clearly recall Grandma's face and hear her ghostly voice telling me to stay alert for these signs. Always vigilant for the opportunities they brought or the warnings they signaled; she imparted their importance to me. So I suspected last summer the months to come would be unusual, not only because of all the predictions of higher than normal temperatures. There was also the low-level anxiety building in my gut, warning me, a rough patch lay ahead.

I recall those quiet drives from the airport to the prison. There were few cars on the lonely two-lane road, just an old pick-up truck every now and then. Life in rural Mississippi moves at a slow pace as there is nothing requiring folks to hurry. Still I remained alert, mindful of the speed limit, not wanting to draw the attention of police. One thing that hadn't changed in my lifetime, the uncertain outcomes of encounters between black men and the law.

One of the last visits I had with Billy stayed in my mind. It was my third visit since January. By the time I arrived at the prison, the sun's rays had gradually burned away the hovering haze, forecasting a meaner afternoon. But the searing humidity did not dampen my enthusiasm for the visit. Being a child of the soupy weather, I knew life made no concessions for uncomfortably high temperatures. Just as I'd also learned early on, unless an inconvenience threatened my existence, it was merely a nuisance to be tolerated for a time. This is a constant life lesson, especially in my professional life.

Approaching the massive complex, my mind briefly, flashed back to the office and the face of one member of the team who was putting my future in jeopardy. Immediately rage and fear coursed through me like venom. With supreme effort I set those emotions aside and adopted the appropriate nonthreatening persona for the visit. *Now is not the time.*

I also remembered Grandma's admonishment, "Always walk with purpose and confidence. Show the world you know where you're going." Even so, I suppressed the easy movements of my body not wanting them to look like a swagger. Once inside the building only the humidity was missing, allowing inmates to tolerate the oppressive heat. As I set waiting for my old friend, pictures of childhood antics flooded my mind, but I held the smile that threatened to escape. We were renegades. To Grandma's everlasting distrust, Billy and I formed, what turned out to be an unbreakable bond.

As he walked through the heavy metal door on the left, he seemed shorter, but that couldn't be. We were always equal in height, over six feet. Sitting across from me, without preamble, he began the conversation as if we'd last spoken yesterday.

"Every time you walk through those doors, I prepare myself for the visit to be your last."

"You know me better than that. Brothers never abandon each other,"

Each of us examined the other with the eyes of our youth, looking for changes in understanding, any hint of disrespect or a fraying of our decades-long connection. I saw only a friendship that held fast, respect flowing freely. Time, itself had bound us together. But I understood the challenge of Billy's often manipulative behavior. Today he projected an air that showed respect for the bond, but also tinged with a hint of superior knowledge. Behind the spoken words, I saw a brief spark of relief in his pale gray eyes. The boyhood smile I remembered was now marred by the empty space where a missing tooth once set. Through all our years, I learned to peel back the layers of his hidden intentions. Our bond never depended on one-upsmanship. He always had my back.

I also saw raw intimidation before he eased into a more relaxed, but watchful posture. I didn't avert my eyes. His threatening stance was not directed at me. It was a necessary skill he needed to survive the prison system. We had chosen different journeys powered by narratives that set like heavy weights between us. But both of us knew the friendship was stronger than the bumps on our individual paths. Billy was born with everything necessary for a comfortable life. He was a bright white boy with an easy-going nature and open smile that charmed everyone who met him. With these attributes he was destined to succeed. Even with his expanding midriff, the promise of youth shone just as bright, but didn't completely hide the intensity of his prison aura: projecting strength and dominance, while never showing weakness. It was terrifying.

The physical barriers now separating us did not limit the comfortable recall of easier times. I began the familiar dance of words. "You didn't know it, but you were my first mentor. My initial understanding of people came from watching you; how you were able to convince us to act on your orders, the expectation your every request would be honored and most of all, your assumption of leadership. To this day when working on solutions, I often ask myself, what would Billy do?"

"Fun days, weren't they?" His chalk-white face briefly flushed with color and his eyes softened, less alert.

"Fun maybe, but wild for sure." I often recalled some of the dark and dangerous games we played. A grimace crossed Billy's face as he quickly raised a hand to his chest. His breathing seemed more labored, something I hadn't noticed during previous visits. "Are you okay?"

"Just a little indigestion." Still holding his chest, he took a heavy breath and continued, "We learned a lot about life, maneuvering through all the twists and turns of our young days."

"Between what I learned from you and Grandma I have almost perfect accuracy on reading people's actions, even yours Billy Cady."

An honest grin swept away his serious expression. For a moment we sat quietly remembering our long-ago small group, running up and down narrow dirt roads. We were a rag-tag bunch that gave no truck to social conventions. Over time the group shrank, but Billy and I stood our ground holding the friendship precious.

We didn't rush the conversation even though I had a late evening plane reservation after a brief stop in Sero. I never let go of respect for his opinion on my life events. Today I was also hoping for some useful bit of information I could take away concerning my current professional difficulty. I'd told Billy during an earlier visit about the investigation I ordered against a subordinate I suspected was engaged in illegal activity. The first time I brought it up, his identity was unknown. Discussing my concerns with Billy was as natural as breathing. I listened with the expectation of hearing an idea that might strengthen my strategy for trapping the person who was putting my life at risk.

"I see you still favor expensive suits."

Proper business attire had been the subject of many of our conversations, even though he had zero business experience. "You and Grandma taught me well. Presentation is everything. The whole package matters."

"Never forget it," he warned.

We set for a while in respectful silence when words neither add to nor detract from the warmth of the brief time together. It was important just to have the presence of a trusted peer. Our alliance had been tested and forged into a bond so tight that no matter each individual journey, the connection remained intact. Billy had offered me a measure of protection, during our most risky adventures. The memory of one horrifying summer night sneaked up on me and flickered briefly in my mind's eye. Even now remembering the attack is terrifying. Billy saved my life that night. Then as time will have its way, I give back to him, visiting frequently.

"Remember Jeremy Cobb?"

"Uh huh, that scrawny kid who was always hungry."

"He passed through here two months ago."

"I often wondered why he hung around with us. He seemed to have more reliability at home than we did, just not enough food. I couldn't figure out how our rag-tag group was relevant to his life."

"You'll always find hidden layers behind a family's outward façade. They didn't have any more stability than we did. Like my father, his dad had another family with three kids down in Jackson. That's where he was when he died after having a stroke."

"How do you know that?"

"You can't be a leader if you don't have all the pieces. I still make it my business to know everything."

Not everything. You can only live in the past. "Whatever happened to Jimmy, Cave and Clem?"

"Jimmy disappeared. I think his family moved to Kentucky. Cave is still living in that shack he grew up in. Clem fell on hard times, worse than my situation."

How can that be?

"He'd kill for those comforts now."

We discussed more of our youthful adventures. No one outside the group knew all our exploits. Billy made our little secret cabal feel we could trust only each other, so we held close. He possessed a natural propensity to provide answers to the many questions and wonderings I put to him, so by habit our conversations were peppered with a question and answer cadence. Finally, he turned to my professional problem. "What's happening with that chump, the one trying to cause you trouble?"

"I hired private investigators and have him in my gun sight. We're tracking every thread of his life, inch by inch. So far his associations in the company have not revealed anything important. But they're going back year by year, to the day he was born. By following his every move, we're getting closer to his scheme. What we haven't been able to discover, is what is motivating him."

Billy's eyes bored into mine. "Maybe who, is the question you need to ask."

This was one of those times when the conversational roles appeared more like father-to-son talks than friend-to-friend.

"The only way to find this person is to make sure the investigators check relatives and friends. Often someone other than the person you've targeted holds the answers you're looking for. Don't forget, it's dangerous to overlook those in your own closet." In the dim light Billy dispensed his usual blunt reality. "Who can you trust with your life?"

"Probably, only you," *Especially now that you're in no position to affect anything concerning me.*

"No one is without secrets, some buried so deep, they hide in their everyday actions."

Even you, my friend?

Billy's slow smile acknowledged my thoughts. We were boys again, shutting out everything around us, strategizing under the limited shade on the side of the old dry levee, one of our favorite spots. Suddenly the heat rose with the tempo of our conversation. Anything, no matter how obscure, that affected my domain as an executive of a global powerhouse, demanded serious scrutiny and Billy was the only person I trusted with my secret fears.

"Never let fear of what might happen stand as a roadblock in your investigation. No matter how frightening the situation appears, if you're ignorant of its scope, you are at the mercy of someone else's scheme." Again, for a moment, we sat without speaking.

"Where have you traveled lately?" He followed my career and knew of my travels to foreign countries.

"Shanghai."

"Must have been an eye opener."

"Not really, it wasn't my first trip."

"How did they take you?"

I knew his question referred to my race. "There's little time available for lessons in race relations when you're structuring a deal. Getting the deal done is the only focus. Whatever shock they experienced the first time I met with them quickly disappeared. When they sit across from me, they don't see a black face, they see a foreign face, one who represents a path to their success or failure. And I see the same thing."

After batting around old memories laced with current happenings, our time together was almost over. The play of the game was to let Billy close out. "Thanks man, keep me posted on the investigation. Remember, this guy has slipped under your radar. Examine everybody over your lifetime and his. Are you stopping in Sero today?"

"Yes, a short stop. You know I like to get back to the airport before dark."

We stood simultaneously. "The next time we meet I'd also like to hear more about how you resolve the conflict of having two women in your life. You need to choose: the advantages of one over the consequential damage of having both of them."

Still maneuvering.

Billy gave one last caution, "Get a better hold on your emotions. You seemed agitated today. That will undermine your attention to the details of the investigation. The color of your skin makes you an easy target. I hope you've not risen so high you now feel like a white man. Dangerous."

I didn't flinch. he was never shy with his opinions and often liked to heighten the intensity of our conversations with outrageous pronouncements. He was, however, reminding me to remain alert. That was not the first time. The initial caution came on a warm summer night several days after he saved my life. The long years never dulled the edge of my gratefulness. "No and I remind myself of that very point on every occasion: at cocktail parties or meetings with the powers-that-be around the world. But there's always that creeping thought that maybe, just maybe, things are different at my level. That's when survival kicks in and I let reality wash over me like a bucket of ice water. It rights my world quickly."

"Good. At your level or mine, nothing has changed, you're still a black man in America."

"So you keep reminding me."

Before he disappeared through the metal door, he turned back as if there was something more he wanted to say but wasn't yet ready. I could tell by his slumping shoulders and especially, the intensity of his pupils. Was I seeing fear, a little less confidence, resignation maybe? These unanswered questions added to my anxious feelings. We'd shared so much. My sensitivity to the give-and-take flow of our conversations, enhanced my ability to recognize the slightest change. He was, of course, weary of the struggle to survive behind bars, but resigned to his fate. His 45-year sentence guaranteed prison would be his home for the remainder of his life. My visits were respite for him. His fear they would cease was unfounded. I would never abandon him.

I was so perplexed by his sad, then playful demeanor during the visit, I eased the car onto the narrow shoulder, leaving the motor running. What had changed for him? The time for Billy to be afraid had long passed and so had resignation which always comes immediately after fear proves itself useless. He'd lived behind bars for ten years. What is different now? Unable to answer the questions, I drove on, shutting off the conflicting emotions. My thoughts turned to other topics we discussed, the two women in my life. Each owned a special place. Whether I should choose was not a priority. It never seemed important enough to exclude one or the other. Kena is the connection to my past and Rita represents who I am today.

I thought of my son's future. Would his life also be burdened by past decisions of others? He should not have to drag around the same baggage I inherited. I want him to explore every mile of his journey. It's the same hope Grandma had for me. The difference is, I know the potholed road ahead, Grandma did not.

As the car moved smoothly through the quiet countryside, I couldn't help reflecting on my early days in Sero. My first encounter with Billy was the second day after my mother left me with Grandma. We met on the side road just off the fork leading in one direction to Grandma's house and in the opposite direction toward Billy's place. While exploring my new environment, I looked up seeing a boy walking toward me. This would become a familiar scene during the coming years.

"What's your name?" Billy asked immediately when he reached the spot where I stood.

"Thomas Jefferson."

"I'm Billy Cady."

For months, he believed my last name was Jefferson. It was only after we started school that he learned it is my middle name. What else was said during that first meeting is lost in time. But day after day Billy and I met on the road and played together until dusk when Grandma called me to come inside. Slowly, as the years passed, I allowed myself to slip deeper into the friendship, even when I had doubts it would last. I could never pinpoint when trust took hold and the doubts began to lose power, but it became the cornerstone of our bond. Neither of us ever stopped testing the strength of our friendship. There were times Billy stretched the boundaries, introducing race into the conversation, but I pushed back. When necessary, we called a draw, just to preserve the friendship. Over time casual friends and even our families paid little attention to our flaunting conventional Mississippi norms: everybody except Grandma Neetha, she never let her guard down.

Being an only child, I had no brother or sister to share secrets or hidden places and never attached to any particular person in the many places my mother and I temporarily lived. So, I huddled with Billy like a brother. He did have brothers and a sister, but they shared no observable sibling relationship. He ignored them and they left him alone. Our lives ran parallel in ways we didn't understand during those early years. Both of us were growing up without the gentle rain of a mother's love.

The frankness with which we'd always discussed everything is one of the reasons we bonded more like brothers than neighborhood friends; nothing was off limits. Shared secrets and reliance on each other filled the void of young boys growing up with the understanding each had to fend for himself. We tended to exclude others. All those years in jail Billy had only me to rely on and I still needed his opinion even on matters he had no experience. He had a way of focusing that helped me clarify certain issues, one was the absence of my mother. For years whenever I spoke of her returning for me, he would immediately ask, "When did you last see her?" This question always brought a small measure of clarity to my continuing confusion about her absence.

Once around age nine we were sitting near the levee, just passing the time when I asked him where could he live if his mom went away? I never even considered he had another parent to see after him, although I glimpsed his father every now and then. Since I had no relationship with my own father, I didn't understand what role Billy's dad had in his daily life.

Immediately he answered, "I don't need to go anyplace, my sister Jenny can look after things."

It was clear his father did not figure in any alternate plan for him. Sero was not a place where fathers left early in the morning and returned at the end of the day, rewarded by compensation at designated intervals. No, this was the town of fathers who faded into the background. In truth Billy was just as fatherless as I.

2

I am 44 years old and live a life of privilege by America's standards. My position as Vice President for International Affairs at Carshale & Berkshire provides boundless financial rewards. I came into this world amid international turmoil. We were exiting the Viet Nam quagmire, the civil rights struggle was strengthening its hold on the country's psyche and women were demanding to have their voices heard, enforced by law. These changes however, had no effect on life in Sero.

As with so many other black men, I live with all the inconsistencies, and inconveniencies of daily life when even the measure of our successes and achievements is often limited by negative racial stereotypes. There are times when my perception of a small indignity by a service person morphs into a challenge I feel must be addressed on the spot. Being on the lookout for such slights and the need to protect my manhood at all costs started early; concern about my acceptance on the first day of school, my look, hair or clothes. Am I like my classmates or different? I remain conflicted about my ability to always handle many of these same indignities endured by men like me in generations past. My body tightens when I approach a yellow traffic light, wondering about the police cruiser parked at the side of the road, expecting a whirling red light to come after me? When someone looks at me, does he see a successful executive or is that person overlaying me with only images of an unemployable felon? How will my son react to threats aimed at his efforts to be a man, threats often accompanied by violence? These thoughts are often ambiguous, but always crouching, ready to spring forth at any hint of disrespect by colleagues, subordinates, peers, even strangers. I've woven them into the fabric of my life, while each day having to affirm my manhood. The continued efforts are becoming more onerous, but I force myself to remember that everything I have can be snatched away from me in an instant, even my dignity.

A week before I was born, my parents having no other place to go, had someone drive them to Grandma Neetha's house. That person stayed a couple of hours and drove off. After my mother gave birth, they stayed two weeks, then we were driven away by the same person who brought them to Sero. I was five years old when we returned to Grandma's. This time I was left behind.

Love hadn't poured out of her at first. Later she adopted a serious approach and accepted the role as stand-in-parent. What little she had, she always made sure my needs were met, giving me my own bedroom at the front of the house while she occupied the back bedroom. No one else I'd ever met slept in a room all alone. Rooms in the cramped homes I'd slept in were always occupied by several people.

Her small house was neat and homey. There was a front living room and behind it a dining room. The kitchen and bath were at the back of the house. She was proud of that house and taught me to feel honored that I had a place to call home. Eventually we became a team. Her hope was to have me avoid all the pitfalls that tripped her own son, my father. Eight months after my mother hadn't returned, her boss, Mr. W.B., helped her gain full custody of me. Grandma believed my mother was what she described as mental, constantly moving from place to place. The only credit Grandma gave her was her luck in not having another child. But to be honest, I was never sure I am her only child. During the infrequent times she came to Sero, names would come up in conversations with no explanation who they were.

When Grandma passed, she left the home to me. I decided not to sell it but to give another struggling family the opportunity to have decent housing as long as they maintained it properly. I had only a short time to check on the house and speak to the tenants before returning to the airport. They needed to know I expected them to keep their side of our agreement.

Drawing closer to the old home place the springs and suspension of the powerful rental car eased my ride over the rutted road leading to the house. Nothing had changed, no pricey suburban developments here. There were a few structures standing on their last legs looking about to fall down: evidence the heirs had abandoned them and moved on. Each one of those houses once had loving and proud owners who somehow managed to scrape together enough cash to buy the land and put up a house: dead and gone with no one left to care and remember.

Once I reached the intersection where another country road crossed, pleasant memories washed over me. Billy and I met here on the way to school. His house was to the left, a half mile down the road. I turned right navigating the large potholes and slowed the car as I approached our house. It looked stable.

I didn't bother to lock the car. There was no one around to run off with it. A potential thief couldn't find this settlement, even with a map. Sero didn't appear on any map I'd ever seen. Walking toward the house, I reminded myself the dirt underpinning the area was ancient when humans lived in caves. But there was a time when its rich bounty helped build a nation while enslaving an entire race of once noble people. The soil knows pain, a small measure of joy, surely hurt, deceit and death. Still, its promise never died. Dust rose clinging to my polished wingtips, soft as doeskin. They represented a new moment in history, modern power. *Maybe someday life here will be different.* The weight of the burden of my future rests in my head, unlike on the tired shoulders of those men who once knew intimately these grains of sand. I need the strength of this ground, the smell and feel of it: most of all I need the memories that built my expectations.

Standing in the front yard, staring at the porch, loving memories continued. *Wow. We did just fine, didn't we Grandma. Everything seems to still be up to your standards.* I'd seen many fine old houses in my travels and those that were still standing, only by the force of love. Our house had the patina of a home that had weathered the years with dignity. I walked up the stairs looking carefully and touched the boards flanking the front door.

No one answered my knock. Then, just as I did on each visit, I walked around the house, checking for any sign of neglect. The tenants understood their part of the bargain, repair or replace any outside siding. I gave them a break on the rent and expected them to keep the property in good order. One small area under the dining room window caught my eye. Taking a closer look, I made a mental note of what appeared to be a loose plank. The house seemed so much smaller than I remembered. Of course, I was now looking with adult eyes. As a child, though, when I had to scrub and polish the floors, the size was enormous.

Still no sign anyone was at home. I marveled at the tree in the center of the backyard. It was a spindly little thing when I came to live here. My job was to keep it alive. "Pull all those weeds from around the roots." I could hear her voice. "When the roots die, a tree has no more life. You remember that. This tree was born one year after you. I don't want to see it gone." I staked it, made sure it had enough water and never let weeds get a foothold. I felt a sense of pride. *Now look at you: all grown up, just like me.* The three chairs around its trunk gave further assurance that this old pal continued to have an important role in the lives of the people who now live here.

I decided to sit a few minutes, so I turned one of the chairs around and sat facing the back of the house, accepting the conflicting emotions taking hold. Now living in a world so unlike Sero, I could if I wanted, block its history from my mind. Everyone told me to get an education, a job, work hard, save my money and I'll control my life. I followed these rules to the letter. Why then am I still so concerned about being disrespected? No matter the boundaries I set in my efforts to control my life, there appears to be no protection against breach of these boundaries by the whims of other men who see me as a threat. Even today, I won't be comfortable until I reach the airport and return the rental car.

Grandma, did you ever think, after so many years we'd still be a part of this place? "Take care of all you have, it'll see you through," she cautioned. My life carries me around the world, but I always come back and make sure all is well here. She put her heart and soul into this home, and we scraped, painted and replaced whatever needed replacing. As I sat continuing my inspection, bittersweet emotions comforted me. Even through, she never attempted to make me promise to keep the house, her serious manner of appreciating every aspect of life rubbed off on me. This place sheltered me and gave me safety.

Since it was clear I would not get a chance to speak with the tenants, I went up the porch steps and looked through the back window. Nothing amiss that I could see.

Before driving out of the yard, I stopped the car taking in the view of the other small houses on the road. I felt a pull to linger, but I needed to be back at the airport by nine o' clock. I drove off, satisfied with my decision to keep the house. I needed these deep-rooted memories to sustain me for the maelstrom that lay ahead. "Don't wait for the snake you know is in the grass to come down the hill. Climb up and sever its head. That way he's dead before he ever knows you're there." Thanks Grandma. It works every time. *So far.*

Continuous memories of Billy and I as young boys clashed with the reality of today's visit. But these memories kept my company during the drive back to Memphis. Behind Billy's cool exterior was his love for details. If I were discussing something that happened the day or week before or the possibility of a future occurrence, his eyes would widen, become like fisheyes. Often, I'd embellish the story just as an experiment. When his eyes widened, I knew I'd not told him enough and during the next visit he'd have an opinion or suggestion about it. An example of the small power plays we carried out with each other from time to time. His attention during our visits was still intense, mostly my stories were the only ones being told. Sometimes I go day by day. He became familiar with the flow and names of people in my professional life. If he were anyone else, I'd wonder how he found time to think about issues in my life when survival in a jungle-like environment should consume his every thought. But I'd come to count on those discussions, as I'd always valued his opinions. I looked forward to the visits just as much as he did.

For the first time in twenty-four hours I was truly still, even in the busy airport terminal. I dialed Kena. "Just checking in, how's the little guy?" Not a day passes that I don't feel the sting of not having my son with me, even as I travel to the far corners of the world. I make sure he wants for nothing: private school and all the other activities he desires.

"He's asleep."

"I'll talk to him tomorrow. How're you?"

"Great. Yesterday I was promoted to head of my department. I followed your advice about the reorganization."

"Congratulations. I knew you could do it. It can be tricky maneuvering through corporate kingdoms." The strength of our unusual relationship held fast with Deon at the center. "I'm flying out to Shanghai next month and plan to break up my flight for a short visit with Deon. I'll coordinate the dates with you."

"How long will you stay?"

Tonight I didn't hear any hidden expectation in her question. Past experience had erased any hope of a different relationship between us. "Two or three days, but you and Deon will have my full attention."

I was not flying one of the corporate jets. Usually, when I come to Mississippi, I fly commercial, putting myself at the mercy of scheduling, so I had extra time. Sitting in the dark bar sipping a gin and tonic, my body finally relaxed, but my mind would not let go of what lay ahead; to take out that traitorous scum. *I know who you are and what you're doing. I know your contacts. When I know the full extent of your game and the others involved, I'll see your asses in hell.* Except for Billy, I kept the treachery I'd unearthed to myself. Carshale & Berkshire is one of the top five government contractors outside of the defense industry and is awash in billions of dollars of government money. Human nature being what it is, there is always the opportunity for fraud and the cleverest person will always find a way around all the checks and balances built into the system. Instead what I discovered so far was not fraud against the company, but someone in my department who is at the center of a drug ring: a dangerous affront to me. If he isn't stopped, I'll lose everything. *I went looking for the snake I knew was there. When I learn more, I will decapitate him.* The drink soothed my rising rage and the unusual quiet in the small room allowed for complete clarity of the challenge I faced back at the office.

3

Flying west following endless sunlight keeps me optimistic, more hours available to reflect on the nature of my relationship with Kena. Even fellow passengers look more hopeful. Being captive in the cabin of a plane for hours allowed my thoughts about her to flow freely. *Kena my love, I need your comfort, your softness, most of all, your unconditional caring. Someday I'll make it up to you, every moment.* Grandma Neetha had her doubts: too forward she always said, just trying to trap a man.

We'd had a brief discussion about marriage before Deon was born and again before his 1st birthday. At the time it didn't seem to be a priority. Not to me anyway, but it never took away my feeling of responsibility to provide for her every need.

By the time the plane set down at LAX and I'd secured a rental car, dusk was settling over the sprawling city. While driving through the endless sea of cars my expected pleasure at seeing two of the most important people in my life, blotted out all thoughts of professional retribution against a snake. The process was still in play.

The spectacular house was cleverly positioned to take full advantage of the site. As with most of the homes in this area, the size of the lot was not extravagant. The views of the hills and city skyline beyond, however, were stunning and represented much of the fortune I'd paid for these three levels.

Kena answered the doorbell immediately, "Forgot your key?"

"No, I didn't want to frighten you." I'd purchased the house for them. It was in her name only.

Suddenly I felt a surging need to feel her in my arms and soothe the exhaustion of the five-hour flight. Her warm body excited my senses. Nothing was said, but the embrace held promises.

"What time will Deon be home?"

"In a couple of hours." She'd let me know he was with friends and would not be home when I arrived. Reluctantly I pulled away. Declining her offer of food, we settled on a soft sofa facing each other in the old comfortable and familiar way of people with an unencumbered history.

"When will you have time to stay for a longer visit?"

The question set off a chain of conflicting emotions. Leaning forward slightly, I looked deeply into her eyes, needing to be sure there were no hidden expectations. "Sweetheart I can't anticipate my schedule for the next several months. I don't want to disappoint you. Any promise I make tonight is one I'm likely unable to keep."

She seemed satisfied and moved closer, resting her head in the cradle of my arm. Nothing else was mentioned about the length of my visit. Time slipped away as we talked about Deon and his daily activities.

"Daddy, Daddy," Deon ran toward me, hugging my waist.

"Hey, little man, what's happening?"

"Daddy, how long will you be here?"

"Until Sunday, we have two whole days together. What do you want to do while I'm here?"

Stepping back, he grabbed my hand, "I don't know, maybe we can go to the zoo." There was a hopeful tone in his answer. "Come and see my turtles," he abruptly changed the subject.

In the far corner of his bright room was a large aquarium with three young turtles resting on rocks. "That's Mo," then pointing to the other two, "and Little Time and Slow Poke." His pride was evident as he described them.

"You'll have two full days with your dad. You can decide the schedule in the morning," Kena said from the door.

Deon's eyes never left mine, "Okay."

After much cajoling and promises, we were able to get him into bed. Even after he fell asleep, I stayed in the room walking around picking up books and toys, then setting them in their proper places. I couldn't tear myself away as I stood looking down at his peaceful face. "You will never need to wonder about my love. I can't see you every day, but you will always know where I am and that you are never far from my thoughts."

As we lay quietly together, Kena tight in my arms, I recalled other nights like this, long ago, when we discussed our hopes and what the future would look like. Tonight, however, I needed her warmth and she needed assurance of my continued promises to her.

"I never question your commitment."

"But I know you're disappointed. The miles that separate us change nothing."

When I was sure she was asleep, I eased myself from the bed and went back to the big open room as conflict raged on. *I won't let you down. I just can't give you anymore right now.* "But, will you ever be able to give her what you know she wants?", another voice prodded me. Grandma had explained in her own way, "The right woman may come into a man's life at the wrong time; before he's ready. Nothing will come of the relationship until he is ready." I grapple with that every day. There is no question in my mind, Kena is the right woman for me. The contrary voice continued. "But will the time ever be right?" I've been able to move forward in life because I am unafraid to take risks, yet I will not commit to a more permanent relationship with my child's mother.

As I sat staring into the night, Rita's face danced before me. I smiled, acknowledging for sure what Grandma's strong opinion of her would be: wrong woman, wrong time, wrong, wrong. The contrary voice would not let me off the hook. "Are you afraid to commit to either of them, next month, next year, ever?" I stand up to every obstacle I encounter daily, but I had no answer. Just one month ago Billy asked the same question.

After so many years, I still rely on the words and logic of my grandmother, but often I wonder if her experiences can stand up to the life I live. My century is so very different from the cloistered segregated society of her times. Every thought she had was colored by those experiences, even my name, Thomas Jefferson Sloane. "Call yourself T.J., it sounds better." I trusted almost everything she told me. Did she ever steer me wrong?

Across the years, her answer echoed with swift certainty. "No."

Back in bed, still unable to sleep, I closed my eyes absorbing the soothing quiet as conflict and doubt disrupted the calm I craved. But Kena slept peacefully. I suspect she'd settled the conflict of her place in my life years ago. She occupied an important and unique place and could hold it as long as she wanted. Marriage between us was still not a priority and would probably not happen anytime in the near future.

I wonder how Grandma would feel about her today. Her advice to me never stopped. She was preparing me for the world she knew, black and white. It's very gray now. Her hope was that I'd rise to the top of black people's world becoming a doctor or lawyer: teach school maybe. That meant following a path already laid out, every curve and pothole set in stone. Without realizing it, her words also inspired me to expect more options for my future. I was able to glimpse a world where anything was possible. I could smell its promise and I planted my feet in that direction.

But with every step I take I must stand my ground. Whenever I think I'm beyond boundaries set by others, the struggle intensifies. Now when I need to make personal decisions, the focus returns to survival. Even with Mr. Fitzgerald's guidance, I couldn't let go of its grip. Now an SOB has made my life a target, but I'll run him through like a knife slicing butter.

"You can never let your guard down," was Grandma's constant warning. She kept an eagle eye on my relationships with playmates and friends. She steered me in the direction where I would see how the world works and make the right choices. She never fully approved of my friendship with Billy but always stopped short of banning it. From him, too, I learned the lesson of the proverbial snake in the grass, crawling low and not making a sound. That skill morphed into my decision to treat everyone as a suspect and saboteur of my life. Good thing. I was put into a snake pit on my very first job. I expected it. That's how the world works. When a newcomer enters the pit, he is walking into an environment in which everyone is seeking domination, but he must walk in and take control when the others least expect an interloper to move in on them. So it is in the corporate universe.

My first experience in the corporate pit was a test. Mr. Fitzgerald wanted an indication of my grit. For the first year he guided my steps through the bureaucratic maze as I began to think differently, to rely on my own understanding of how to proceed and make only the decisions that supported my choices. I continued to benefit from his guidance in resolving professional issues for years, even after I left the company. We became personal friends and I still touch base with him whenever I think I need to. He admonished me early not to use race as an excuse. I was not astonished or surprised, it had also been one of Grandma Neetha's tenets for survival, though given reluctantly. "Stick to your plan. It'll be a long time coming before some people can see beyond your blackness." Even so it adds to conflicts and ambivalence in many other parts of my life, including the possibility of a more permanent relationship with either Kena or Rita.

Despite being awake most of the night, I rose early. Deon and I spent most of Saturday at the zoo. He was mesmerized by the huge turtles barely moving near the rocks in their enclosure. "Will Slow Poke get that big?"

We spent all day doing only what Deon wanted. I allowed him to consume as much ice cream and other sweets his mother would never permit. After the zoo, we went to an outdoor restaurant and ate more iffy food. My opportunities to indulge my son were not as frequent as I would like. Our time together was all that mattered. Soon enough Kena would have him back on a regular schedule. His memories of our weekend will last forever. Something I never had with my father. It was after nine when we returned home.

4

Even as we prepared for take-off on the long flight to Shanghai, I remained vigilant for any surprises concerning the upcoming negotiations or new information from my private investigators. As flying time wound down, fears of ancient prejudices and unacceptance seeped into my calm. The trip was fraught with danger. These unsettled emotions brought deep feelings of uncertainty as I wondered if the person trying to ruin me could undermine the goals of this trip. Restless, I walked down the aisle talking with the other members of the team. The group exuded confidence and a subdued measure of excitement. The hours droned away and finally I slept, waking a couple of hours before touchdown and began mentally reviewing each step of the planned negotiations.

Arriving in Shanghai at 2 A.M. did not dim the team's enthusiasm. They'd slept only in short spurts during the twelve-hour flight. As I stepped from the plane my senses spiked to high alert even though I'd dealt with these people for months. There were other face-to-face meetings in New York. But with them, every word spoken had a double meaning, often hiding the truth under layers of speech. Once we cleared customs, our driver quickly deposited us at the hotel. After a few hours' sleep and breakfast, we went over the presentation again, then left for our meeting. As always Shanghai was bustling in every space available. People did a delicate dance as they jostled for room to pass each other. I saw more cars than during previous trips and drivers constantly honked horns in a never-ending desire to move faster. This hustle and bustle added to our excitement. Every building seemed to be reaching for the clouds, the skyline getting taller and taller. Shanghai looks like New York City on steroids.

The meeting room dazzled. It was large with a bank of windows covering an entire wall. The antique rug covering most of the floor was designed with an ancient pattern; pale cream with a blue dragon sailing through the middle. The antique vases sitting atop the chests against the wall behind us were priceless.

Once the meeting started everyone in the room breathed as one. Negotiations with these people started years before our current team took control. Not so, the Chinese. Each one of them had been involved from the beginning. We were confident we'd reach an agreement which both sides would find acceptable. Tension decreased, but all parties retained a high level of alertness. At the end of the day we returned to our hotel and immediately reviewed the day's events. We could find no holes in our position. As part of the preparation we'd considered the most salient points of opposition the Chinese would put forward at the very beginning of negotiations.

"We'll reassemble in a couple of hours and preview tomorrow's meeting." I never considered we'd have an early night. There would be no rest for them until we were over the Pacific on the return flight home with a solid agreement.

"Right," Greg added.

With pots of coffee to steel us against weariness, we forged on. The team had prepared two charts: one containing their goals for the trip, the other showing the goals we met today. Greg drew lines through the accomplishments. The agreement with the Chinese must permit unscheduled inspections of all financial documents of the new acquisition by people our company selects. This was a tough nut, but not an impossible achievement.

"We arrived as adversaries, now we must make them part of our team. It's time to move up a level. Just as we were, they were also wary entering these negotiations. It was noticeable how they slowed us down each time we considered an issue settled. They'd require one more review. Every time Mr. Chu interjected the rule of referring matters to the ministry, that was to remind us the deal is not done until they feel they've squeezed us as hard as they can without the process breaking down."

"I understand the process, but my research shows that when Mr. Chu sends a proposed agreement to the ministry, it is never rejected."

"Good. You understand then. He has let us know who holds the winning hand. We know he does. We enter tomorrow's discussions with less distance between our positions. Mr. Chu will not hit us over the head with the ministry again, he's made his point. At each stage of tomorrow's negotiations, you must point out their particular position is no different from ours. You demonstrate this, point by specific point. Make it clear we want the same conclusion they want."

"That is the precise goal. They don't want the kind of publicity that might frighten investors. By coming together in a unified agreement both sides can support, we really do want the same protections." Greg showed impressive confidence.

Weary to the bone, we finally stopped for the night at 11:30 P.M., however I reviewed the process one more time before crawling into bed and falling asleep immediately.

We were a much more subdued group on our return to ministry headquarters the following morning. The assembled Chinese greeted us with an exaggerated sense of enthusiasm. No doubt they too had had a long night. Even though they were moving to the conclusion they sought, our team remained respectfully alert, permitting the Chinese to continually remind us of the rules that apply to foreign companies. We recognized this intimidation tactic. What our company wanted could only be granted by the men sitting across from us. This reality was our guiding light. Greg moved the negotiations forward and pulled back as necessary. My trust in his capability was rewarded with his masterful performance. *But his smile is just too damn wide.*

Mr. Chu drew most of my attention. His facial expression never changed, but I watched for other signs of what he was really thinking. He usually kept both hands on the table with his fingers threaded together. Whenever he made a steeple of his index fingers and began to rub them together, I knew we'd touched an important point. He also began to shuffle his feet. It was only at these times Mr. Chu interjected himself into the negotiations, which alerted me to take charge of the team. We were prepared for tedious negotiations; therefore, no one attempted to rush the talks.

After a short lunch break, we resumed discussions and at the end of the day, had resolved only two issues. So that the team would remain alert, I decided they should take the evening off and review matters early the next morning after a good night's rest. We needed to put brakes on the Chinese strategy of wearing us down.

The early night worked wonders for the team's enthusiasm. We began the third day of discussions with a stronger sense of purpose. Our goal was to close the deal by the end of the day. After the morning greetings and handshakes, both sides faced each other with hard determination. When Mr. Chu's fingers started to move, and his feet began their shuffling motions. I permitted myself an inward smile, holding back any outward show of emotion.

By two o' clock each side had grudging respect for the other. We'd pushed hard to reach agreement on the final issues. The tension in the room lessened slightly.

Just as we began to tackle the last hurdle to agreement, a clerk entered the room and handed a folded note to Mr. Chu. He read it, handed it back to her and nodded his head. She walked around the table and handed the note to me.

Emergency, call Kena immediately.

5

Six hours after we signed the agreement, I was on a plane to Los Angeles. The remainder of the team would leave for New York the following morning. I went straight to the hospital upon arrival at LAX.

The entry doors slid open silently. The bright-colored two-story reception area was designed to put patients and their families at ease the moment they entered. With receipt of a visitor's pass I rode the express elevator to Deon's floor and without hesitation entered his room, quickly absorbing the scene. But for the medical equipment supporting the tubes and other implements necessary in a hospital room; it could have been Deon's own room. Bold blue and orange stripes along the wall complemented the window treatments with chairs in the same hues.

I had so many questions, but I didn't want to worry her. However, when I entered the room, I couldn't contain myself. "Has there been any change?"

Kena turned, relief on her face. "No."

Quickly giving her a hug, I leaned over Deon's bed examining him carefully, even lifting the bed sheet from his legs. There were tubes plugged into his body and I could hear the hum of machines doing their life-giving work.

"I assumed you would return to New York before coming here."

"Oh no, nothing comes before you and Deon. When did his condition worsen?"

"Two days ago, he became listless, just lying around on the floor. He had a headache and vomited a few times. I didn't think there was anything wrong, except he may have been playing hard and was overly tired. But he began to move less and less, so I called his pediatrician and she had me bring him in immediately. Before we could leave the house, he slipped into a coma. I called an ambulance and he was brought here."

"What do they think has caused this?"

"A brain contusion."

"Did he fall or hurt his head?"

"You know how active he is, he may have fallen, and I was unaware of it." As she tried to explain, she lovingly brushed her son's face as if these gentle touches would miraculously cause him to open his eyes.

A nurse came into the room and efficiently checked all the tubes. "Nothing has changed," she told them, knowing they were hoping for any information that would bolster their hopes. "The medical team will meet in the next hour. After their consult, we'll be able to get a better prognosis. If you have any questions or concerns, push the button and someone will come immediately."

Once the nurse left the room, we set on each side of Deon's bed watching him with intense certainty that he would at any moment wake and smile at us. For the remainder of the day our frustration alternated between parental longing, that never gives in, and hope for a miracle.

At set times doctors and nurses came in to check on him and offer comforting words. His breathing remained steady.

After many hours waiting for patience to reward us, he opened his eyes briefly. After several more hours I decided it was best to go home and return in the morning. He was peaceful. "I'll drive my car and follow you." I arrived ten minutes after Kena. Walking up the steps, the sense of calm I usually felt, whenever I entered the house, was absent.

"I made a drink for you. It's on the kitchen counter," Kena called from the top of the stairs.

"Thanks." As I moved to the back of the house, again, as in many other times, I was seduced by the scene through the wall of glass opening before me: the setting sun cast a golden glow over the rugged canyon beyond. Easing myself onto a deep sofa, for the first time today I thought about the China agreement. Before leaving I'd directed the team to take a day off for relaxation before beginning implementation of the agreement. They'd worked aggressively for weeks and would be rewarded for every hour spent on the project. Each would receive top bonuses for the team's performance.

A soothing sip of the rich scotch and water slowly released the tight grip I'd held on my emotions as I began to relax. When Kena joined me, for the first time, I noticed the drawn lines around her mouth. Quiet settled around us; words were not necessary. Our fearful thoughts were on Deon. Would he be lost to us? The nagging possibility would not go away. But it was imperative I comfort her as she tried to hide her fears. "We must believe he'll be okay; the doctors are doing everything medicine allows." I felt some of her tension ease.

Once we were in bed, I took her in my arms, holding her close. The same beautiful canyon scene from the first floor unfolded through the wall of glass in the bedroom. For these few hours we'd release our cares to each other.

Carrying the heavy weight of hope, we took separate cars to the hospital early the next morning. Deon's breathing was still steady, but his eyes remained closed. "Why don't you go on to your office. I'll call you If anything changes."

I felt paralyzed standing beside Deon's bed. The nurses suggested I talk to him. They explained, there are cases where a person in a coma sometimes awakes and begins a conversation concerning bits of words heard while in the deep sleep. Keeping an even voice, I began my story using words a young boy understood.

"On the day you were born I made a vow to you; I would never abandon you or your mother. I know the stinging heartache of not having access to a parent's loving time and attention.

Of course, you know I grew up in the home of my Grandma in Sero, Mississippi. I was just six years younger than you when I went to live with her, even though I was born in her home. We came by car with friends of my mother who were driving up to Memphis. It wasn't a long ride, but there were so many people in the car, I sat on my mother's lap the entire trip.

When we arrived, I learned later Grandma Neetha didn't even know we were coming. Looking back, I don't believe she would have allowed my mother in the house if she had come alone. I think my mother knew that.

The first thing out of Grandma's mouth was, "What are you doing here?"

"And hello to you too Ms. Neetha," was all my mother said, while climbing the porch steps. I scrambled up behind her.

To my five-year-old mind nothing seemed out of the ordinary for us. We'd stayed in many different houses. But because the car we'd arrived in had left, I thought we would be there for a short stay. I didn't know at the time, but my mother and grandmother had enough history that they knew each other's limits.

My mother carried our two bags into the house. Grandma directed us to put them in the first bedroom.

"When did the little fellow eat?" she asked, referring to me.

"Before we left," was all my mom said. Her answer left Grandma to decide for herself: not giving a complete answer protected her options.

During our initial days in Sero my mother mostly set on the porch. At other times she took short walks down the road and back. Grandma Neetha and I slowly got to know each other. She asked straight questions and I answered with as little explanation as required. My early life with her rarely included small talk. We spoke what needed to be said. She talked mostly life lessons. She was taller than most women, with wide shoulders, which added an air of authority to her words.

Two weeks after we arrived, my mother left. I was confused because usually we had only short stays at the various places that sheltered us, then we'd leave together. I would not see her again for three years.

6

I could not be sure Deon heard any of the words I spoke, but talking to him was something tangible I could do beyond waiting for him to open his eyes. I began again, recalling the memories of a little boy who never developed a proper relationship with either the woman or man who brought him into the world. Whether they loved me, I don't know. But you will not have to go through your life wondering about my love.

After my mother left, Grandma Neetha began the process of mothering me by first explaining the house rules. I paid attention, listening for each nuanced word. I was accustomed to observing how things were done in the places I'd lived. This was the first time anyone paid enough attention to me to actually describe how I should conduct myself in someone's home. She watched me trying to learn about life. An uneasy peace existed between us at first, because I thought my time with her was limited and so did she. We, therefore, moved around the house like temporary roommates instead of close relatives.

You're probably wondering how a child my age remembers so much of those early years. There's no mystery to it. Like any child who begins life moving from place to place, with no permanence, I became a really good observer of people and situations. I learned to read faces and accurately predict behavior: a skill that serves me well today.

On my second day in Sero I met Billy. Our friendship began with back and forth questions about each other and the honest responses only five-year-olds can give. "I don't know" was my only answer to questions about my mother. The getting acquainted behavior went on for a few days before we began to play together, just the two of us, mostly kicking a ball around.

Our fast friendship was grounded in easy interaction with a lack of need for either of us to out-do the other. We were two boys with no toys. The ball we kicked around belonged to Billy's brother. One day he came without it and after sitting under a tree, he suggested we go down to the levee. We were expanding our territory for the first time. Because I was a solitary child, I didn't wonder or ask why we didn't include others in our budding friendship. There were other children in the area. In time I came to know some of the black kids at the tiny church Grandma attended. But, none of them visited me. Billy was my only playmate in those early days.

Years before Grandma and even the Cadys arrived, the county organized itself in a way that cut Sero out of any planning, leaving the town to rise or fall as it was capable. The people were encapsulated in a cocoon and shunted aside. Forward moving blacks had gone north years before. The whites were left in limbo, waiting for something to happen, anything. Each group knew the rules, so there was never any friction to speak of. Everyone was just hoping to make one more day. In our rural community, for young people, the separation lines became bolder and blacker as we moved toward adulthood.

Being acutely aware my time with Grandma was not intended to be permanent and my mother's continued absence, I gradually began to believe the length of my stay might lay in my own hands. I just needed to follow house rules. I then forgot my self-imposed probation with her, allowing myself a kind of freedom from fear of this unknown extended stay. But my belief she had the power to send me away for any misstep always rested in the back of my mind.

Telling my story to Deon released the tense knots in my neck and back. I pulled the chair closer to his bed before continuing.

Days turned into weeks with no word from my mom. As time passed, I looked for her beautiful face and quick smile. Whatever a person wanted, my mother's smile said, 'got it.' It was that potent. I also needed to assure myself she hadn't changed her hair. She had long, thick hair that sometimes looked black and at other times appeared to be a wine-brown color. Her skin color was just right. She had a very level temperament. I never saw her angry or out of sorts. Looking back, I can only believe she used her looks and devil-may-care demeanor to move us around. After a month with Grandma Neetha I stopped looking for her everyday. Something else I learned early on; pay attention to my present situation, learning to live in a new and different place.

By the time school started, my mother had not come for me, therefore Grandma registered me for my first grade class. It was then I began to interact more with other children in the area. The new friends did not, however take from my odd friendship with Billy. My teacher, Ms. Tucker, had the same tendencies as Grandma. She allowed no breach of order in her classroom. Even Billy capitulated. With our amenable friendship we naturally became friendly competitors. On occasion as we walked to school three or four other people walked with us, however Billy didn't encourage it. I think both of us wanted to keep our close ties exclusive. Certainly my need to have my own friend, who was always available, never slackened and Billy was a reliable companion.

Weeks after school started, we'd heard nothing from my mother. Thanksgiving came. We took our food to Grandma's little church and celebrated with other families. Her turkey was the largest and tastiest as everyone said to her. The special seasonings she used to flavor her dishes accompanied her to the grave. While clearing out our house, after her death, every woman from the church asked to have her recipes. I never found any written evidence of how she prepared the cakes and pies she produced in a heartbeat. They had to satisfy themselves with lesser remembrances: a fancy glass vase or one of the many what-nots she treasured.

Anyway, as my first Christmas in Sero was approaching, still no sign of my mother. Grandma and I were of one accord, albeit unspoken. We planned for her unexpected appearance by including a gift for her under our small tree. Christmas came and went still no word from her. I didn't realize it, but I was settling into a new circumstance, family living. The predictable structure of school grew comfortable. I followed school rules, even as reality conflicted with the facts. At any time, my mother could arrive and take me to another temporary home and school.

Before coming to Sero, I'd had only brief experiences with learning, but I knew my numbers and alphabets. Grandma went over new words with me every night until I knew them perfectly. It was harder for her to help me after third grade, so she found someone in the church who could assist me. These efforts paid off. The teachers saw my potential and pushed me. It made Grandma Neetha push even harder. She liked to say, "Your best isn't good enough, it has to be my best." For years to come, I lived by that mantra. As an adult. I watched the behavior and habits of others who made important decisions and considered the actions that worked for them and those that slowed their progress. I adopted their winning methods and then went beyond their levels. It always works.

I felt good going to school. I owned the process and never missed a day. Waking up at the same time everyday, I dressed myself and ate breakfast. Grandma left my food on the stove, covered with a cloth napkin. She left early for work in Mr. W.B.'s house, walking a half mile to the paved road where he picked her up.

There were periods lasting a day or two when I didn't think about my mother, but mostly I operated under a shadow of uncertainty, not knowing when I would have to move on. In June I was promoted to the second grade. There was no summer school available, therefore I had more time to consider my future with Grandma.

As I talked to my son, many long-forgotten memories of those early years in Sero floated to the surface. I only stopped my narrative when staff came in to care for him and didn't realize how quickly the hours had passed until Kena returned. "Any changes, any at all?" She saw his closed eyes, but her mother's heart asked anyway.

"Nothing. The doctor was here twice but could not offer any more information than he did this morning."

Kena took one of Deon's hands into hers. "Baby, this is Mommie, I know you can hear me. Open your eyes and tell me what you want to do this weekend. Would you like to go to the aquarium? There are new animals."

I watched her, feeling helpless, knowing we would need extraordinary patience. He was receiving every treatment available. We could only wait and continue talking to him.

My own childhood longings blended with my hopeful visions for him as I gazed on his silent face. "I can't leave here until I see his eyes and hear his voice." Abandoning them was unthinkable. I dialed my assistant. "I'll be back in the office when I know Deon is on the road to recovery. Cancel all meetings for the next three days. Decide what is urgent, and if necessary, I can communicate from here."

The strained look on Kena's face caused me a brief feeling of guilt.

I owe you so much more than I can give now.

Still holding Deon's hand, her fingers locked with his. Raising her head, she looked at me with questions in her eyes.

"He will come out of this. I promise. His breathing is steady. In time he'll open his eyes and we'll have our son back just as he was before." I put as much assurance in my voice as I could muster.

As hours slipped by, we set next to his bed, hope resting between us like a reliable friend who is always available when needed. I finally convinced Kena to go home for some much needed rest. "I'll stay and call you immediately if there are any changes."

After she left, I sat down and thought of the child never born. We'd lost the baby by miscarriage. In an instant he was taken and so could Deon. He too could vanish into a mere memory. My heart almost stopped, just as I felt again the feeble movement of his fingers. I returned a gentle squeeze and continued my story.

Between remembering my early years and telling the story, I was removed from the hospital room and cast back to the house in Sero where dreams were scarce. Without Grandma's efforts, it would have been easy for our dreams to die quickly or dribble away slowly.

"The years were long before I knew Grandma's story: the reasons she often appeared distant and cold. I would learn, her youth was hard. She suffered, not only at the hands of the southern racial system, but her own family gave little solace and support to a young girl who was too tall, too dark and lacking any personality that would get her noticed. So she embraced the ignored place she occupied.

From one year to the next I continued to live with conflicting feelings about my mother. Grandma didn't often mention her name. I believe she made a conscious effort not to bad-mouth her, but for sure, she never expressed a complementary word. Billy, on the other hand, asked many questions, but never expressed a negative opinion about her continued absence.

When I saw my mother again surprise and shock struck me at once. One day as I neared the house, parked in the front yard was a heavy dark blue car. My heart began to beat faster. I knew she had come. At once my childhood resolve not to go with her shattered like glass. I was eight years old, in the fourth grade and had not seen her for three years.

"Is this your mom's car?" Billy asked, running his hand along the side of the car. Over time I'd continually explained to him, she would come for me

"I don't know, but she's here."

Both of us stared at the car. I felt like a cornered rabbit. Even though I'd declared to myself, I would not leave with her, a feeling of sadness swept through me. Would Grandma let me go if she asks to take me? We stood in place longer than reasonable for a boy who hadn't seen his mother in years.

"Aren't you going in?"

Just at that moment Grandma opened the door and waved, summoning me. One step at a time, I went into the house.

My mother stood and came to me." Sitting at the end of the sofa was a man. He must be the owner of the car. "You're a big boy now, so tall."

I nodded my head in agreement. I didn't know what words she wanted from me.

"Cat got your tongue?"

I still hadn't found my voice. She placed a finger under my chin and tilted my face upward. "It's been a long time, I thought you'd be glad to see me."

I hunched my shoulders. It never occurred to me she might really want me to be with her after leaving me behind for so many years.

"He's surprised to see you, that's all," the man on the sofa spoke.

He'd given me an opening, "I'm surprised."

The beautiful face I remembered, smiled. "I hear you're in the fourth grade; are you good with your school subjects?"

"He's at the top of his class," Grandma Neetha said defensively."

"What's your favorite subject?"

"Math, but I like reading too."

"I guess I should have brought you some books."

"I have books." I told her, hoping she would not think I was missing anything important. "I'll show you." I went into my room and quickly came back with several of the books my teacher had given me.

As I was laying them out on the small table, I dropped a couple. She reached down and picked them up.

"I'm sorry." I was anxious for everything to be okay.

"How long are you going to be here?" Grandma Neetha wanted this issue settled.

My mother turned to the man at the end of the sofa, "We'll play it by ear," he responded directly to Grandma.

"Well let's have something to eat. Change your clothes T.J. and get your chores done."

"I'll go and tell Billy to go on home." He was still standing by the car. "I can't come out now, my mom and her friend are here." I hadn't been introduced to the man yet, so I didn't know his name.

"Will she be here tomorrow?"

I couldn't tell if he was hopeful for me or disappointed we would not be able to play. "I don't know."

"I'll see you in the morning," and he walked away with slumping shoulders. He was never anxious to go home.

"I'd been outside only a minute, so everyone was still in the living room when I returned, but I went through to change my clothes. Grandma went into the kitchen where I soon joined her.

"Ms. Neetha, is it okay if we sit on your porch?" my mother called from the front of the house.

"Help yourself."

The front door closed loudly, and Grandma immediately turned to me and said, "Whatever you're thinking, remember this house is your home."

"Did my mom say she was taking me with her?" Dread and hope battled for dominance in my mind.

"The only thing your mother asked was, where is my baby. It never occurred to her that you would be in school. When I got home, she and her friend were sitting on the steps. No surprise she'd shown up after all these years. People who move in circles always end up again and again at the same points in their lives."

I didn't understand what she meant; had she been looking for my mom to come back? As she began preparing our meal, I went out back to take care of the garden. It was my job to water, weed and do whatever was required to grow the plants. Like everything else on the premises, the garden was clean, orderly and well-cared for. Most of the vegetables we ate came from that compact patch of earth. Grandma canned as much as she had room for and gave other jars to church members with larger households. I was taking longer than usual to complete the gardening chore. Any conversation I might have with my mother didn't come to mind as I was afraid I'd say something that would cause her to take me.

Vacillating between the five-year-old she'd last seen and my eight-year-old self, I concentrated on what I could do to get my position heard. Would she understand how proud I feel having my own room, friends and a family, even if it consisted only of Grandma Neetha? All I knew about my mother was that she moved around frequently. She swept into my life after not one word in three years. Did she now have her own house to take me? Who is this man with her? What was her life like these past years? Has she seen my dad?

Who could I depend on to help me if I decided not to go with her? Does Grandma Neetha love me enough to fight for me? My teacher, Ms Agnes: if I run to her house, will she keep me? The Pastor? Finally, the answer came to me. Of all the other people I thought of, I knew I could depend on Billy to help me hide from her. A sense of relief settled over me just as Grandma called from the kitchen door.

"You've finished out there?"

"Yes." I walked slowly toward the back door.

"Go sit with your mother." As she turned, I heard her say under her breath, "And see what she's up to."

Walking around the side of the house to the front, I sat on the top step and turned sideways so I could look at my mother who set in the chair nearest me. I was still reluctant to have conversation with her because I wasn't sure what I was expected to say. But she opened the discussion about our missing years.

"Did you think about me?"

"Yes. I often wonder what you're doing as you travel around and who are the people you're living with.

The man whose name I did not know yet, made a sound between humor and disbelief. "Humph."

"Do you ever talk to Daddy?"

She was silent so long I thought she might not answer, but finally she responded, "Every now and then."

"Where is he?"

"In Ohio," was all she said before changing the subject. "Sometimes I find a job and make a little money." She opened her purse and took out a small tube of folded bills. "I saved a few dollars for you." She got up, leaned over taking my hand and placed the money into my palm. She then closed my fingers around the bills.

"A late Christmas present, you can count it later."

"Where were you at Christmas?"

"Which one?"

"Last year."

She looked at the man next to her and smiled. "We were living it up in Georgia, had a good time too."

An unexpected feeling of sadness washed through me. "Were you in Georgia every Christmas?" I'd imagined she might call and wish me a Merry Christmas.

"No, different places."

I understood. She was still moving from place to place. I'd found my home, but she hadn't been as fortunate. Even though I was only eight years old, I decided at that moment I would not leave Sero with her. I'd run away first, knowing Billy would help me hide.

I wondered if she went back to any of the places we stayed when I was with her. What about those people? Memories of them had faded, but I wondered anyway.

"Supper's ready," Grandma said, as she opened the door.

I waited until my mom and her friend went in before I followed. Grandma always sat her table, even when only the two of us ate there. But this evening it had an extra shine.

Grandma suggested my mother say grace, but she deferred to her friend, "You say it Lee."

For the first time I heard his name. After grace he became more talkative. Maybe my mother met him while working one of the few temporary jobs she'd had. I surreptitiously thought there was something special about the way she looked at him. She looked proud, lips slightly parted and with a glimmer of hope in her eyes. A spasm of jealously passed through me and I couldn't help wondering if she felt proud of me too. Was she proud that I obeyed Grandma's rules, had my own room, went to school every day and did all of my homework? Most of all was she proud I was a good boy? I needed to know how she felt about me.

During a lull in the conversation, I decided to tell her about my life in Sero. I sensed she would not know how I spent my days if I didn't tell her myself.

"I help Grandma with chores around the house"

"What do you do?"

"I take care of the yard and garden."

"And a good job he does too." Grandma added.

"I keep my room clean and I polish my shoes. Sometimes I clean the table after we eat, and other chores Grandma needs me to do."

A twinge of disappointment swept through me when she made no comment. I wanted her approval.

Quiet settled in the room as we ate. For the remainder of our meal, not wanting anyone to notice, I glanced sideways at my mother, wondering about her plans. Where is she going from here?

We went back to the porch after eating, but Grandma stayed in the kitchen. I summoned every bit of courage I could muster, and blurted out, "Where're you going?"

Again, she looked at Lee and he responded, "Chicago."

"For how long?" I insisted.

My mother spoke up. "Why do you ask? Do you want to come with us?"

"No, I'm staying here with Grandma Neetha."

"You're sure?"

"I live here." I needed to express ownership of my situation. Nothing more was said about my living arrangements. Grandma joined us a few minutes later. About nine o'clock, my mother and her friend drove away. A strange sense of safety settled on me. She was gone, nothing had changed for me. Even so, I experienced a brief feeling of disappointment. When I saw my mother again, I was no longer a little boy afraid of any actions she might take.

In the coming years Grandma and Billy kept my hopes alive for a future beyond the confining triangle connecting our house, Billy's house and the levee. But it was only from Grandma that I learned, while looking toward the future, I must consider unintended consequences that always shadow hope. The wrong choice of friends, lack of education or not grabbing opportunities that show up unexpectedly, could derail her hopes for me. She knew the sting of possibilities being crushed in an instant. It was only with Billy, however, that I could share my conflicting fantasies of reuniting with my mom.

I did nothing to upset Grandma. During all the years we lived together I kept my antennae tuned to her requirements. She was patient and I remember how clear she always laid out instructions for the smooth running of our home. Her clarity developed in me the ability to focus, sometimes to the exclusion of everything except the task directly in front of me. In the world of business, it serves me well.

Caught up in the tale of my youthful memories, I almost missed seeing the slight flutter of Deon's eyelids, but I heard the weak moaning sounds and gently squeezed his hand in response. Again, he quieted, and I returned to the story.

The years rolled on with little change in our lives. Grandma was stern in her expectations. She'd had a life full of challenges and knew intimately hard times: the look, smell and hidden traps of struggle. She hadn't had the best education, but deeply understood its importance and the necessity to steer me through the rough seas of youth; a time when many young men begin to self-destruct. She would make one more try to turn a boy into a man. She had many rules. The first rule, during school nights, I was to be in the house behind closed doors when the sun goes down. Only a school activity she'd checked on, allowed an exception. Any infraction would let her know I wanted to live somewhere else and she was prepared to send me to live with an uncle in Cincinnati, in a house with five other youngsters. Since I was the only young person in her home, she thought I should appreciate my special situation.

Whenever I think back to those days, I see in all aspects of my life she was right on target. When it came to proper dressing she cautioned, "You always present yourself in the manner you want people to receive you. Put those clothes on for tomorrow's work. Who do you want to be? Tomorrow is today." She never allowed any adventurous haircuts. I still keep my hair close-cut.

Her ideas about success in life came from her observation of the success of the man she worked for, Mr. W.B., as she called him. I finally understood her reasoning and it fit with Billy's approach; people believe what they see. No matter where I am, my appearance never undermines the vision I have for myself. In the boardroom, office, golf course or restaurant, it has to speak authority and demand respect.

She'd moved to Sero from a down and out town in Alabama by way of a brief sojourn in Ohio. She was the only girl in a family with six children. At any time, there were four or five other people living with them, sitting and sleeping in whatever space each claimed and could hold. It was, I later learned, in that smothering environment her modest dream began to form. "I just wanted a room of my own, one I didn't have to share."

Grandma constantly worked to distinguish herself as different, someone special, who if she tried hard enough, could make me special too. She never mixed love with survival. Each had to stand alone. "Talk of love," she said, "softens a person, confuses responsibilities. The person loved, knows it. There is no need to pronounce it at every turn. But survival, that's another matter. It has to take precedence over everything else, especially true in our dusty, forlorn backwater. If you wake up every morning planning to survive the twenty-four hours in front of you, you'll make it to the next day."

I thank you Grandma Neetha, survival thinking has taken me to the top. Without it, I could be just as irrelevant as Billy, now only passing time, going nowhere and worse. It was the only lesson I needed.

Throughout my childhood and teen years, the hallmark of her efforts to assure my survival, was to keep her eyes on all my friendships, including the girls who sniffed around, as she described it. Billy and his family were always under her microscope. In addition to his brothers and sister, his father's brother's family were living in and out of their house for two or three years. He didn't seem to be attached to them. They were rarely invited to join us on our adventures. There was an invisible line between him and those nomadic cousins. He exhibited a superior attitude toward them which they accepted without complaint. He was never mean, just ignored them. We hooked school a couple of times, just to hang out at the levee, doing absolutely nothing but having endless discussions about every aspect of our limited world. He could talk his way out of any misadventure and always protected me from the actions of the other boys who were envious of our close friendship. Frequently my situation may have turned out differently if I had not been one of his crew.

The soft knock and opening door stopped my narrative. The doctor came in just as Deon began to struggle, turning his head from side to side. After examining him, he explained Deon was coming out of the coma.

Good news at last. "Does it mean we can take him home soon?"

"We'll see how he responds. Right now, we don't anticipate any setbacks."

Deon's recovery was remarkable. I stayed on for two days after his discharge. We hired a private nursing service to provide care until he could return to school. Kena didn't need to miss days from her office, just as she started a new position. But a sense of shame descended on me as I drove to the airport, wondering whether Deon longed for me to stay or take him with me. Was he suffering the same conflict I experienced when my mom left me with Grandma? On a moment's thought, once I reached the airport, I changed my flight to route me through Memphis. I needed to hear from the last person alive who remembered that time. Billy will help me sort through these conflicting emotions comparing my childhood with Deon's.

7

"How are things at home?" Rita and I have been together for more than five years, yet whenever she speaks of my home, her reference is always to Deon. Her habit of looking at me directly had taught her how to gauge my feelings and emotions. Since returning, I'd been distracted: physically with her, but mentally somewhere else.

"Deon is recovering nicely. All is well in Sero. I could find no fault with the tenant's care of the house, on the outside at least."

She wanted my full attention. I'd been on auto pilot during her phone calls. Her concern for Deon's health scare was genuine and I never hesitated bringing her up to speed about all that was happening in his life. She hadn't met Deon, but she'd seen so many pictures of him, she felt she knew him. As to Kena, we never discuss that part of my life.

"And how is Billy?" A safer subject for her.

"He was more reserved. I can't put my hand on the reason, it's just a feeling I have. He's still seriously concerned I may stop the visits. It puzzles me because I've never postponed any visits with him. I wouldn't abandon him like that."

"He knows how demanding your life is and probably feels at any time you would need to scratch a visit."

"Only if Deon needed me."

With so much traveling, I always look forward to returning to the office with its predictable routine. I think of it as having a utilitarian soul. Everything needed is there without appearing cluttered. The windows face south, bringing in the early morning sun, flooding the room with bright light and giving me a feeling of warmth and welcome. Usually the view is calming, but this morning anxious feelings crowded out this peace. Was there a difference in Kena this trip? And Billy, there was a definite aura of finality about him. Something was off. How could there be any changes of consequence in his life with his circumstances? What does Deon truly think about me? How long will Rita stay in my life, without the promise of more? These questions wouldn't let go even as I sat at my desk.

With great effort I focused my attention on the matters in front of me: conference schedules, emails and return calls my assistant left for my direct attention. Also, there were stacks of paper I needed to review before the afternoon meeting with the China team. I started plowing through them, shutting out everything else. Each sheet received laser scrutiny, being well aware that lack of focus had brought down many men. Finally, these matters were behind me and I joined the group.

Wrapping up the afternoon meeting I felt a sense of satisfaction. It was important for these young people to present the precise process they considered appropriate for the new division expanding in China. Most executives at my level would not spend this much quality time with younger up-and-comers, but I did not arrive at my level by doing only what was considered appropriate for top tier. I'd received unexpected opportunities on my way to the top and vowed to work with aspiring leaders. I enjoyed the hands-on approach when mentoring.

I personally selected each member of this young team and chose only those who had my vision and the ability to focus relentlessly on its achievement. I met with them often going over their plans, watching them come together as a single cohesive unit. They'd grown more comfortable voicing unconventional ideas. Constant attention allowed me to get into their heads and play the role of devil's advocate, asking detailed questions at every meeting, insisting they think like an executive of a different culture. They role-played in the way of litigators: testing plaintiff's position against the opposition. They worked well together, trusted each other's opinions and were able to immediately spot any holes in the plan. They created a brand that allowed them to recognize challenges and creative paths to overcome them.

Greg led this seven-member team with an impressive measure of boldness. His talent, and work habits mirrored my own. With the suggestions he'd made, the plan was solid. As the leader of the team he and four others would accompany me on the return trip to Shanghai. Watching them as they left the room, I was pleased with the unity and respect they gave each other.

Once again, I was required to move forward knowing there was a fork in the road ahead. As much as I admired his professional talent, Greg was now my nemeses, but I never let on he was the target of the secret investigation. He'd been identified by the investigators. I walked a tightrope. The time to burst his bubble was coming closer, but for now I'll hold him close. I must do nothing to let on I know his game. If he has to be replaced as leader of the China team, so be it. I asked him to stay behind a minute. "The strategy you set is perfect. You started with a tough, but realistic goal and developed a super efficient plan. We leave in two weeks."

Hours later my thoughts drifted in an angry cauldron at the real possibility that I could be drawn into a web of criminality just because of my position in the company. By the end of the day I was still moving what was left of the pile of work that met me hours earlier. I'd made progress and was determined not to leave the office before completing every task needing my attention. When I finally left there were a couple of other people also reducing their workloads.

Daylight had faded completely by the time I reached my apartment. A soothing drink accompanied by a delivered meal eased, only slightly, the unsettled mood that had attached to me. The chatter in my head quieted finally as I fell into a fitful sleep.

The next morning, I awoke with a clearer head. Since I was no stranger to uncertainty in my life, I knew the current predicament with Greg, was not to be given short shrift. I needed to remain calm and not allow my emotions to tip him off. Again, the internal argument began to assert itself, however I cut it off. *This is only a distraction. It's not about me.* The voice would not shut down quietly, *but this man's treachery is directly about me.* This unreasonable fear would not leave me. At stake was my life of climbing, never looking back, until now.

I set at my desk and began to reread the report. It was spare, but covered all details: He appeared to be working alone. There are no other employees in the company involved. We're still searching, however. Money is not a problem for him, as you know he is supremely compensated.

His family is an enigma. Parents have a history of moving around frequently. Even his siblings have little stability. There are three brothers and two sisters. He has not visited these people in the last five years. Records show he sends a small amount of money to them infrequently: approximately $200.00 to $300.00 every four to five months.

His money, most of it, goes to fuel his lifestyle. He isn't flashy, but spends unlimited funds on parties, clothes, of course, the car, a couple of women he's involved with.

His friends are mostly people he's known since college and business school. There are two friends he seems closer to than others. We're checking their backgrounds also.

I was so caught up in the report, my secretary was inside the room before I looked up. "You have a call from California."

I reached for the phone immediately, knowing it was Kena. "What's up?"

"I carried Deon back to emergency last night. His temperature rose to 103 degrees. He's okay now, just wanted you to have the latest information."

"I can be out there by daybreak."

"That's not necessary. I'll keep you updated on his condition."

I was anxious to touch my son, to hold him. *I must find a way to have him with me more often.*

~

Between keeping tabs on Deon and overseeing the company's global responsibilities, I had little extra time for anything else. The investigation into the criminal in my immediate team was moving briskly. We needed additional information before making the decision to unmask and arrest him.

"Be merciless in going after him and taking him down." Billy had advised. "Your life or his. Take your choice."

There was no one inside the company I trusted to strategize and give honest advice on this threat. I vacillated between anger and a sense of victimization with my position being undermined by someone who has nothing to lose. I have my entire life hanging in the balance.

Why, then did I not seek Mr. Fitzgerald's help? Early in my career his direct intervention smoothed so many bumps in my path. He supervised my first internship and helped me get my first job. Always honest, he took the time to review my reports before they were submitted. He is a wise man and knew the challenges I'd face. My written work needed to withstand the extra scrutiny it would surely receive. He did not hold back as he explained matters of race and survival in the corporate environment. I was a threat to the established order. Of course, I knew I'd meet barriers because of it. Mr. Fitzgerald knew the tactics: disrespect of my position at any level; making me feel I didn't belong with attempts to isolate me and degrade my decisions. "You must leave no doubt that you have command of the moment, be it in a written document or one given orally."

But Mr. Fitzgerald was not carrying the weight of conflicting expectations. Men like him were sure of the possibilities available to them. While I, on the other hand, must constantly worry about shattered dreams.

Just like Grandma, he cautioned me to stay in survival mode, while still encouraging me. "Don't be afraid to advance your position at every step. Strategic self promotion is an important part of the life blood of advancement."

I was already working for the company when he took me to lunch one afternoon and gave me, what he considered his most valuable advice; a principle that is never taught in business school. "Professional advancement is all about balls: who has the biggest balls at the table. And you, they will try to decimate yours. Just remember, the proverbial target is not on your back. To those who oppose you, your balls will never be big enough or white enough."

I've never forgotten the sting of his blunt words. Even when I left the company, he facilitated my first position at Carshale & Berkshire. Yet, I remain conflicted about approaching him with my current situation. Instead, I place more reliance on what Billy thinks. Why does his understanding and advice have more value to me than Mr. Fitzgerald's? Even now I feel a smoldering sense of shame. Is my manhood still threatened? If I bring this up with Mr. Fitzgerald, will he think I'm overreacting or just out-and-out stupid? At this point in my life I don't want to feel I'm on my knees begging him, a white man, for help, even though he unselfishly guided me through the maze of corporate rules, spoken and hidden that enabled me to have the success I enjoy today.

The soft sound of a closing door allowed me a brief respite from the tumultuous emotions that disrupted my ability to relax. The expectation that calamity was just around the corner if I let my guard down for a minute stuck with me like a bad smell. To always remain calm was my constant goal.

To show any level of anger was not an option available to me. I still remember an incident at the beginning of my career when someone stole a promotion from me. My assistance and mentoring of a new employee led to that employee getting the promotion I was sure belonged to me. While simultaneously maintaining a level attitude and bearing the humiliation, the hurt and lack of understanding rattled me so badly I almost left the company. Eventually I did. Mr. Fitzgerald advised me, "Don't take it personally. This type of personnel hiccup often happens in organizations. There will be times when you'll want others to forget about your race, but you must never forget it."

That lesson stripped away any lingering belief I had in the fairness of merit. Nevertheless, I owe him my position today because of all the advice and guidance he gave me.

8

During my May visit with Billy, among the many topics of our far-ranging conversation, the discussion turned to his warm feelings for Grandma. He remembered, what he described as, her kindness to him. "She treated me the same way she treated you."

"What?"

"Lately I've spent time thinking about this. Not once did she ever make me leave your house. When it was time for me to go home, she would address you and say things like, 'It's time for you to get ready for bed' or 'You haven't finished your chores.' And she always let me eat dinner or lunch with the two of you."

"She was always cooking something. Why wouldn't she share? You were my friend."

"Outside my home, I never had a meal anywhere else but your house. At my house we had to scrape together something ourselves. My sister would pull together a sandwich or something. Most of all, Grandma Neetha didn't treat me like trash."

We spent most of our days at my end of town. He was comfortable in my neighborhood. As it turned out, I was the only person who offered a challenge to him. The friendly tension between us kept each sharp. Thinking about his feelings of gratefulness and sometimes referring to her as Grandma instead of Ms. Neetha, caused me to peel away more layers of our childhood. While I was trying to avoid being sent from Grandma's, Billy was attempting to enjoy a sense of family routine with us that was missing in his own home. He wanted stability, just as much as I did. I had the hallmarks of a stable life, even as fears of being sent away stayed with me. During those early years of our friendship we never played at his house. We'd pass by the house on one of our many adventures, but never stopped. His sister and mom were usually sitting on their front porch. They always sat to the left side of the porch, because the right end sloped slightly downward.

I asked Grandma if she knew his family. She said, "I see them at the market."

"Do they go to church?"

"What for? They don't need to ask God for anything."

I didn't think I needed to ask God for anything either, I had a place to live and was slowly losing some of my constant fear of having to move on. Still every Sunday we asked for God's blessing. I had no understanding of what she meant. "Will they be saved?" I pressed her.

"Salvation is for people who breathe only hope. Before our time somebody put hope and salvation in the same bag, shook it up and put it in the hands of people like us. All we know to do is hold onto the bag and learn to believe that one day, we can open it and find something sweet inside."

Not making the connection between my question and her response, I put it aside. But she was not ready to let go.

"My family had no idea where to look for salvation. They thought God had abandoned them or was hiding in a bottle of whisky or even under a women's skirt. They gave up hope and salvation in this world and instead settled for passing time on someone else's piece of the world. They worked like the animals we all once were, to complete another man's hope."

To me hope with salvation was church talk. Every Sunday Pastor Richard constantly talked about holding onto hope.

"What does that mean Grandma?" She remained silent for several minutes. I wasn't sure she heard me.

"We live in hope for better times. My family didn't have a clue how to hold a dream they could not touch. But you need to learn how to make your way in this world. Salvation is in the hereafter, but life stares you in the face every day and you'd better have more than hope to help yourself through to the next day."

"But you always tell me God will give us salvation."

"God takes care of your salvation, but you better take care of every step you make. Don't ever forget it. The minute you step out of line, you may not get another chance to put your hope forward."

I knew she was telling me something important. Just what, I wasn't sure. Always aware of what I considered my fragile place with her, I put forth extra effort in understanding her take on the important lessons to be learned about life. She gave them liberally, often wrapped in stories about herself.

One soft July evening Grandma and I sat together on the front porch staring at the road blending into night. At first there was no conversation. Grandma was secretive about her early years and rarely talked about her life before settling in Sero. When she did, it was often after she sensed a conflicted situation I encountered. As a young girl she worked hard in school and hard at home. She followed all rules, learning everything the teachers presented. To keep up with her studies she volunteered to help her teachers clean the classroom after the other students left. This was no idle decision. She'd thought it through and knew she could get extra help in as little as thirty minutes during this precious time alone with the teachers. Once she returned home, helping to prepare dinner and other chores occupied her until bedtime.

Moving from grade to grade, she made herself even more invisible, quietly observing everyone. Grandma began to think of a plan for her life, dreaming of place of her own. Her plan, she knew, could not evolve in a place that didn't give a damn about her. She would have to leave. But there was no part of the plan that would show her how.

She had no close friends, even though she was surrounded by siblings, cousins and neighborhood youngsters her age. But Grandma's inward-looking nature didn't allow for close emotional interaction with them. The other young people left her alone to develop her own interpretations of their lives. She learned to read people by their actions, their inverted smiles and whether they held their shoulders straight: forward curving shoulders meant the possibility of hidden truths or more likely, lies. Shoulders held back from a chest that appeared puffed-out meant arrogance or an out-and-out fool, presenting too much information about himself.

Grandma was always clear about the issues she relied on to power her life. Not one time did I encounter ambivalence in the principles she used with me or her clarity with other women in our community. By piecing together, the words she left unspoken, I perceived unresolved issues concerning her relationship with my grandfather. She rarely mentioned his name nor did my father during the brief times I saw him.

"Grandma, how did you get to Sero?" As far as I knew she was the only person who chose to make Sero home.

"By the unexpected grace of God." To explain her answer, she returned to a time of deep hurt, remembering statements made to her. "You are not the brightest flower in the bunch, but you can hold your place among the others by establishing the habit of outlasting them. As they wilt, you continue standing until you are the only one left. They appreciate you then." Her father's words were meant to encourage her. He confirmed what she already knew. For her life to move forward she needed to work harder than everybody else. This she did each day, no matter how difficult the challenges. "How can I explain my journey to you?" she asked rhetorically.

I thought she would begin again with her church talk. That seemed to always be at the front of her mind. Without shame she told me her story using only enough words to give a clear picture.

"The people I worked for had a so-so marriage and their situation helped me."

"Mr. W. B.?"

"No. The couple I was working for while I was still with your granddaddy, who was trifling and could never work long enough to get a complete paycheck. I had to take care of us. I wasn't making much, but it was sufficient.

I was looking for a way out, a sign or some chance that things could change. So, I just worked harder, looking for that chance. And it came out of the blue." She hesitated a moment before continuing. "I was off most Sundays, unless they needed me because of some function they were having at the house. I got up one Sunday morning earlier than usual. I couldn't stand the smell of liquor on your granddaddy. I dressed and went to work, let myself in and went straight to the kitchen. I didn't think anything of it when I heard a noise upstairs

They were arguing again, only this time I could hear furniture crashing against a wall; then a piercing scream. The kind that means terror visited to the human body.

"Neetha, help me, please."

At that moment the terror gripped me too and I was paralyzed. The pleading for my help came again followed by the clear sound of a body hit. I ran up the stairs and confronted broken furniture and Ms. Allie flat on the floor. The scene was like a fight between two animals, with the biggest one standing, waiting to continue.

"Help me," she moaned again.

Without thinking I went to her and attempted to help her stand. In a heartbeat Mr. George pushed me with all his fury and I landed on the floor beneath him. I was confused, not understanding what had just happened. This man, when he hired me, was specific; my duty was to make life easy for his wife. She should not have to lift a finger, he told me. That morning as I tried to help her to her feet, to comfort her, I became the object of his bullying, so I just lay back staring up at him. She nor I moved. We held our breaths, knowing the force of the wild power looking down at us. After what seemed forever, he left the room and Mrs. Allie began to whimper, sounding like a wounded dog.

I immediately saw myself in her situation; helpless, powerless, without a port in the storm. I lay on the floor, seeing myself screaming for someone to care for me, to see my need, to help me.

Her continued pitiful moans spurred me to action. I struggled to get her to her feet, then to the bed.

When Mr. George left the house, we were relieved enough to speak. "You okay?" I asked her.

"Call Ann and tell her what happened," she told me. She was calmer after speaking with her sister. I helped her to the car and drove her to the other side of town to be nursed by her sister. As we expected, two or three hours later, Mr. George came for his wife. Her sister and I stood back as he screamed at her to get downstairs and come with him. When he'd cowed her sufficiently, she rose from the bed and stumbled toward the door. I'd seen this interaction between them before. She expected him to come, but the usual way they handled these conflicts was she'd make him work at it. She knew the exact point she would give in and it gave her a measure of satisfaction.

This time though, things didn't go according to the usual plan. When we came down the stairs, just at she reached the bottom step, with me one step above her, he hit her with his fist, right in her face. She fell back on me with her arms flailing. The agonizing screams summoned her sister who started down the steps just as Ms. Allie's hands went to her face. He twisted her hands and pulled at them, preparing to hit her again. Trying to protect herself and push him away, she scratched his face. By now her sister was directly behind me. Mrs. Allie pushed back against me trying to make herself smaller. Her sister's weight was pushing me just as hard from the rear. Automatically, I was still trying to protect Ms. Allie; I tried to pull her to the side of her husband so she would not be in his direct line of fire. I had never seen him this bad. He was now yelling and calling her every kind of bitch he could think of.

Three women on one side and a lone drunk man on the other side. To this day, I don't know how it happened, but with his forward momentum toward his wife, my elbow caught him squarely in his left eye and the pain caused him to fall backward. His anger then turned on me, "Nigger bitch, you hit me, I'll kill you."

For an instant I didn't understand what was happening, unconnected thoughts collided in my head. When he threatened, "You'll pay for this, you will pay." I knew what he meant. I was now caught in the net holding all his hatred and meanness. I gagged on the bitter taste of fear collecting at the back of my mouth. Gently I lowered Ms. Allie to the floor, quickly moved passed him and ran from the house to the car and drove off. I drove the car to their home, parked it in the yard and ran home. There was nothing to leave behind, my little change purse was in my pocket. Only later did I understand I had breached an important boundary I didn't know existed. Even though I was hired to make life easier for Mrs. Allie, that didn't include help against Mr. George's fists.

It was Sunday afternoon. Everyone who lived in the house was home. "I must leave; Mr. George will kill me." As I explained what happened, each knew what I had to do, leave town immediately. My cousin, Arutha said without hesitation, "Joe will drive you to Cincinnati."

We knew our place in the world, so we acted accordingly. Ancient memories of survival took hold. I would have to run as so many before me had done, never to return. By nightfall we were nearly at the halfway point, having driven five hours before stopping for gas. We had sandwiches to ease our hunger. Joe ate, as he drove. We travelled on through the darkness and arrived at my aunt's house early the next morning. My family would deal with Mr. George when he came looking for me. It wouldn't be immediately; his pride must be soothed.

I had to leave your father behind. I knew my cousin would take good care of him. For weeks I remained unsettled. I just couldn't seem to find a niche for myself in this new arrangement. I knew my place at home in Alabama. Life in Ohio was different. People were able to work more hours and often differently, but I only knew how to clean other people's houses and sometimes work in the fields. In Cincinnati there were so many people, my presence did not fade into the background as I was able to do back home. My aunt helped me find work cleaning hotel rooms. I worked with a team of people instead of alone as I was accustomed. My focus and conduct at work were noticed. Soon the others left me alone which permitted me long hours, without interruption, to probe the uncertainties of my situation. I knew Cincinnati would be temporary and I needed another place to make a new start, but I didn't know how I would leave and where I might go. Returning to Alabama was not an option. I adjusted to my life in Ohio because I had to. When not working, I kept busy doing chores for my aunt around the house. This helped me move beyond the nightmare I left behind in Alabama. My aunt understood the predicament I faced was not one I chose. She promised I could stay as long as necessary.

My actions were tied to the rhythm of my aunt's life, including church every Sunday I was not working. It was after a Sunday service that I first heard about Sero. A visiting preacher from that area grabbed my attention as he talked about the church dinners his small congregation shared after service every Sunday. It seemed like a nice quiet place, just the opposite of Cincinnati. Something deep nudged me to ask more about it. It was an out-of-the-way place I could make a new start and be left alone. I went up to him and asked questions about this tiny town. How do I get there, I questioned my aunt latter in the week? She helped me through her church and a woman in Sero agreed to rent me a room. I saved what little money I could and by early summer I was in Sero. The trip required two buses. The first day after I arrived, I went door-to-door until I found a woman whose maid had just the week before, suddenly left for Chicago. I was hired on the spot. It was then that I began to build a life for myself where all the decisions were mine to make; no more drifting on the edges of other people's lives.

Sero turned out to be just the place Grandma needed. She could set her expectations at the level she chose. The only residents in this town were people who lacked the knowledge that a road had transformative powers if you had a dream. Grandma brought her dream with her in every pore of her being. Sero people were stuck in place and unlikely to notice her. Her inoffensive and unobtrusive nature would assure that.

She never came to grips with the reason my grandfather chose her. To her dying day she couldn't trust any explanation that she thought of. "I didn't have the right looks to attract a man: I was too tall, not enough hair and not a big talker. Even more perplexing was why I succumbed to his attentions. I'd seen him around town but had no interaction with him. One fine Saturday outside the store while I walked home, he smiled and spoke to me. Surprised, I stopped, looking at him suspiciously. 'Hi,' was all I said before moving on. The following Saturday he was sitting on the same box in front of the store. He was one or two years older than me and had dropped out of school to work in the fields. Saturday mornings ended his work week. For the remainder of the day he took up residence outside the store that was the general meeting place of the neighborhood. Like men in our part of town, he sat waiting for anything to happen or nothing. I was merely a distraction, even though I didn't know it or maybe I did, but women will always take chances with a man. That's our nature."

My father was born less than a year later. Grandma's life didn't change much, just the additional burden of a child. Hard work being her lot in life, she did what she had to do, adding the care of an infant without complaints or the appearance of any regrets.

"What happened with my father? Did he come to live with you?"

"Twice."

"Why didn't he stay?" Over the years I'd noticed she was reluctant to talk about him, so I wasn't sure she'd answer. When she began to explain she leaned toward me like a conspirator.

"When I left Alabama there was no discussion of him coming with me. I was running for my life, fleeing southern justice. When I ran home that day, I knew my existence was forever altered. My family took charge and within hours I was gone. Len was only four. He would be cared for by my relatives until I could send for him." Grandma's voice was clear and her tone deliberate. She hadn't forgotten any minute of this part of her life.

"I didn't see him again for five years, but I sent money for his care every time I was paid.

Eventually my family sent him to me with relatives who were traveling to Chicago. He was quiet and sad. Life for him in Sero didn't have the excitement of a house full of busy people. During the day I left him with an older woman, so our time together was limited. After several weeks I was not able to soothe his sadness and rouse his interest in living with me. My cousin, who stayed in touch during his time here, suggested he come back to Alabama. She thought the change was too abrupt for him, so she came for him herself. We tried again three years later, but nothing had changed, so he returned to the family he knew.

I continued sending money and writing letters. He, in turn, sent me cards on my birthday and Mother's Day. As the years passed, both of us accepted the separation and no longer made attempts to live together."

"And you never went back to Alabama?"

"No. That part of my past was closed to me. To be honest, sometimes I feel grateful for having had the luck to leave Alabama, as painful as the reason was."

"How can you call running for your life luck?"

Without hesitation she answered with pride, "It gave me this dream and eventually, you."

I'll forever remember the joy she always expressed in having her own home.

"Finally, I saved enough money to buy this home. I didn't have enough to pay the full price, so I needed a mortgage. The bank would not give me one, but my boss loaned me the remaining amount I needed and deducted it from my pay."

9

While keeping her eyes on Billy and me, Grandma Neetha never interfered as long as I held my end of the friendship. There were times, however, she needed to give me a lesson. One of those times occurred one day as a group of us played in the overgrown lot at the corner. It was an unusual occurrence because we'd included some other boys. The group suddenly turned and headed down the road. Billy turned to me and said, "You can't go."

"Why?"

"Only we can go."

I stood there waiting for an explanation. Grandma called me into the house and without ceremony, said, "There are things you can't do, even though Billy can do anything he pleases."

"We were just going down to Caleb's house. His uncle is there."

"Caleb's uncle is the law in these parts and you better always stay away from white men carrying guns." That was it. She didn't make her statement any better or any worse trying to soften the explanation. His uncle didn't live in Sero but came around every now and then.

As time went by, she put it all together for me, "White men shoot us for practice."

A long observer of people, she had to teach me about the ways of life. I needed to understand Sero was not an example of how the country was run. "The minute you tell a boy, who thinks he's a man, he can't do something, he becomes obtuse with the only goal being to oppose what he's told not to do." There was no man to enforce her instructions, so she had to be fierce in not sugarcoating life as she knew it.

She was preparing me for a future she could not envision. But she knew by experience, to reach that future, I would pass through the sometimes long dark tunnel of survival. She didn't direct my every move, although I always felt her shadow weighing my everyday actions, especially around Billy. The years slid by, uneventful and unchanging, until the year of my fifteenth summer. That too was a very hot summer, much warmer than usual: one of the reasons, over time, I've learned to be wary of extreme heat.

At the end of one of those hot days we were still roaming about, not ready to go home. Daylight reluctantly let go of its hold. Earlier in the day we passed time playing at our favorite place near the levee, running on the road and through neighborhood backyards, not a care in the world. The night was soft, and the nocturnal insects buzzed around peacefully. It was a playful evening that allowed our imaginations to flow freely. School was out and we had extra time before going inside for the night. That summer night was one of those moments in a boy's life when time stands still, a perfect moment meant only for carefree pursuits.

Usually only Billy and I decided the direction of our play. We were the acknowledged leaders of the scrappy group whenever we allowed others to join us. I was the only black boy. We'd gone a tad far afield with the intention of putting a scare into Billy's cousin, Jeb, and his girlfriend. We sneaked up on them as they lay on the ground next to the levee. They were lit by a perfectly round moon. Only Billy knew they would be there. I was right behind him as we silently crept up the side of the berm. Then, like a pack of animals we roared across the top and down the other side. The two people lying together on the ground completely naked, jumped up with primal fear on their faces. Billy ran past them taking a stance behind them shouting their names at the top of his lungs. I, on the other hand, stopped and stared in mortal horror. I had never seen a naked white woman. To be truthful, I had never seen any naked woman. My eyes didn't deceive; she was totally without a stitch of clothing. Once they realized they'd been found out they scrambled for clothes while keeping their eyes on me. The other members of the group had run back to the top of the levee and were staring down at the scene below. I was still standing there not able to look away. The girl stood gripping her clothes glaring at me. That image would haunt me for years to come.

Billy shouted, "Let's go."

As one, everyone began to run down the length of the levee. I was the last to leave. For the remainder of the evening I could not get the image of that girl's pale body out of my mind. It came unbidden, to me for days after. When I was alone, I'd sit and picture her smooth whiteness, like a marble statute. And sometimes I became the boy standing with her at the foot of the levee. I didn't know it then, but that image was imprinted onto my mind and there it remains.

~

Days later as I was walking home about ten o' clock, I heard heavy footsteps and looked around. At first there were only two of them, Billy's cousin and a boy I'd never seen. I kept walking.

"Hey."

An electric tingle of alarm quickened my heartbeat. When I turned again, two other strangers had joined the first two. Billy's cousin who, I last saw stark naked, was one of them. All my senses began to vibrate with fear.

Before I could blink, an arm circled my neck and I was in a chokehold having difficulty breathing. With one hand, I pulled on the arm around my neck, I used my other elbow to jab the chest at my back. The hold around my neck weakened slightly, but held hard. In a blink, I knew I could only free myself. I was alone. I raised myself and bored my heel into a knee. He grunted.

With every ounce of strength, I could muster, I wrenched myself free from the vice of the chokehold, knowing I had only seconds. The danger was unimaginable. Before I could make a complete turn, an immense punch pounded my nose. The pungent smell of blood filled my senses. I began to claw at the face in front of me. At the same time, I felt fist after fist as punches pounded my face.

I needed to hold my own before the others joined in, but time was not with me. I punched back landing a few hits to his middle. One on one I could have taken him. I knew what this vicious attack was all about and the hatred behind it. My eyes were stinging and beginning to swell. Giving into my fear was not an option. Survival took hold. I knew I must put whatever space I could muster between us; it made me more maneuverable and gave me a chance to swivel around and land punches of my own. A knee to his groin gave me the space I needed. With Herculean effort, my fist connected with his jaw and when his head snapped back, I went for his eyes, then his nose. Blood and spit flew into my face, but I kept pounding his face with short quick hits, not allowing him to gain traction. Then a teeth-shattering blow landed on the side of my head. Tears mixed with blood and sweat clouded my vision, causing me to stumble. The others had joined the beating. Blows rained down on my head and upper body. I staggered but held my footing.

Alone and outnumbered, my will to survive pushed me to stay on my feet and keep punching back. Feeble as they were, my efforts to land blows on them continued, but I was losing the ability to remain upright. Raw fear heightened the smell of blood. Shocked, for the first time I realized this attack was not a fight to even some perceived misstep, they were trying to kill me. The tiny flame of survival grew like a brush fire burning out of control as I wrenched myself free, unsure where to aim my blows. These were not people who had experience in fighting; neither had I, but I had the will to save my own life.

"What's wrong Mac, you can't take this nigger?"

Vicious blows rained down on my upper body. They were pounding me remorselessly. The pain felt like burning sticks. I only remained upright because I was surrounded. Even so, my arms tried feebly to return a blow, to land a strategic hit. As my swelling eyes diminished my sight, the smell of alcoholic breath directly in front of me, guided my hands as I clawed at the face, while simultaneously again connecting my knee with his groin. He emitted an ear-piercing scream and the smell of alcohol immediately receded. The crushing blows to my ribs seemed to go on forever; waves of spasms convulsing every fiber of my body. There was no sense I had improved my position because the next blow to my head knocked me to the ground. Gasping for air one minute and moaning with pain the next, my hold on reality was slipping fast. I thought I was going to die. Before I lost consciousness, a voice coming out of the dark mist of pain called my name as I was being kicked again and again.

After a week of emotional confusion, the physical bruises began to heal. It would be many more days before the scab on my forehead dried and dropped away. Billy was finally ready to talk about the attack on me. We were sitting in the backyard under my tree. The start of the conversation was no different from all the others we'd had. Without prelude, he went to the heart of the issue.

"I should have told you the rules."

"What rules?"

After a moment's hesitation, he threw up his hands, "Women rules. They cause trouble. If you don't know that you'll end up dead, especially around here. Stick with those girls at your school."

"You mean black girls?"

"That's right."

"Why are you telling me this?"

"Because you don't understand. White girls are not for you."

"You think I don't know that?"

"If you did, you wouldn't have been almost beaten to death. You'd better be glad I came to rescue you. This is something your daddy should have told you."

"You know he hasn't been here. I think he's in Ohio."

"Well I'm telling you, around here you don't stare at a naked white woman." Billy went on fleshing out the rules. "We know what you're thinking about, all her whiteness." His eyes narrowed as he continued, "so smooth and soft."

"You're nuts."

"I know, because I've seen her naked before."

"What?"

"Oh yes, they go behind that part of the levee all the time. I sneak up there and look any time I want to."

"I wasn't trying to see her; it was an accident."

"That accident could have killed you."

Grandma remained silent as the scars faded. Then she put her take on the beating. We were sitting facing each other at the kitchen table. She leaned close. We were eye-to-eye, so close I felt the warmth of her breath. "Down here a white girl's value is determined by who is looking. To a white man her value increases with the intensity of a black man's interest: most times just a look at her. Now for a black man, she's worth what a white man says she's worth. Never forget it. When that girl went down to the levee, she was trash to that boy. When you looked at her, she became golden. You're smart in school; take this learning to the rest of your life."

10

Day by day the years passed. I left home for the first time in late August, heading for college. My scholarship paid for everything. It was not a long bus ride to the small college near Cleveland. As I boarded, Grandma whispered, "I'll miss you. Our plans are unfolding as we hoped." She was proud. It showed in her eyes. But I also saw relief on her face as the bus rolled away.

College was serious business. It never left my mind the reason I was there: to leave in four years with a piece of paper that gave me sure claim to outright ownership of my future. Hard work became my master. But there were times I missed the relaxed talks with Billy and often fell into the habit of comparing the different personalities of new friends with his way of detailed thinking and behaving.

My adjustment to living in the close quarters of a dormitory was not difficult. From my earliest remembrances, I was required to adapt rapidly to limited living spaces I had no right to claim. Having lived all my life being constantly aware of my actions around others, I quickly grasped the requirements of this new environment. I needed to juggle my interactions with many more people and situations than I did in Sero. For the first time I developed close friendships with other black men, who shared similar hopes and dreams.

I noted our differences too: one being their visceral feelings toward 'white people.' The pejorative nature of the term was not part of the endless discussions Billy and I had, so it stuck with me.

I also carried with me the image of my mother's beautiful face and smile that, even as a young man, kept me clinging to the hope of one day feeling the warmth of her love. As an elective, I selected psychology 101 thinking I would find answers to my questions about the reasons she continued to hold herself from me. Had I done something wrong and leaving me behind was punishment? After I'd bent that idea into impossible shapes that didn't hold up to scrutiny, I debunked this explanation. But I continued to twist theories to fit my hope for understanding her behavior.

I never laid eyes on her during my college years, but Grandma had word from her every now and then. She was still moving around. Evidently Grandma let her know my location because several times I received a twenty-dollar bill from her in the mail: not a word, just the money. Each time it also brought surprise mixed with frustration. The questions would begin again. What is she trying to say? Without answers, I convinced myself when the time was right, she would tell me herself, but that was never to be. I finished the psychology class with the highest grade but had advanced no further in understanding my mother than I had at the beginning of the course. I received word two years after I graduated that she'd passed. She was already buried when Grandma informed me. She died in Chicago.

~

Whenever I returned home during short college breaks, Billy and I hung out together as always, having endless conversations about life, mostly mine. During the summers I found work on my college campus, but I managed to come home for two weeks before the next school year began. We took up where we left off sitting under the backyard tree. He wanted to know everything about my life on campus. I was excited sharing the day-to-day details with him. He had a ravenous appetite for every detail and was fascinated with all the new information about, black people. He knew no other blacks than those who lived in Sero and I was the only one who brought back knowledge of a different black life. The details amazed him. The idea of blacks living differently from the lives he saw in Sero was something he never imagined. They were mostly tenant farmers, maids and day workers. He didn't understand why they needed college for those jobs. Even the idea of having different teachers for each subject intrigued him. "Why would you need so many teachers?" The racial make-up of college professors was something else that fascinated him. All of our elementary school teachers were black and of course in our different high schools the teaching staff reflected the reality of life in Sero.

The most intriguing idea of all to him, was my revelation that black men had secret groups. When I explained college fraternity life to him, all he said was, "I like that."

"Who would you include in your fraternity and what name would you give it?"

"Must the name be Greek?"

They were the only ones I'd ever heard of, "Yes."

I didn't know at the time, but our discussion that day may have been the start of his criminal journey as he began to put together the idea of forming his own secret fraternity-like organization. I, of course, was not included in any aspect of his plans. When I learned he was in trouble, our lives had diverged for more than two decades.

Interacting with so many different people, I felt the need to change my distinctive southern accent. However, it was that accent that bought Kena into my life. She was standing nearby one day when she heard my voice and teasingly commented. "I bet two dollars you're from below the Mason-Dixon Line."

"And you would hit the jackpot."

We became fast friends and eventually more. My feelings for her were strong and irrational. The girls in Sero were more reserved and knew their places. College girls, on the other hand, operated from positions of equality. These women challenged me with their bold and often brash statements. Kena was super smart and also attending under full scholarship.

By the end of the second semester of my second year we were known as a couple and our relationship survived the summer break with the exchange of letters. Grandma didn't have any information about this looming situation until I returned home for the short break. During the next two years we became closer. Once out of college we initially went in separate directions but continued to hold the strong bond we'd created earlier. Eventually we reconnected at a deeper level.

Years passed before I stopped comparing Kena's every action with my mother's. I was to challenge myself many times over the years before I understood it was only my perception of her, I was clinging to. Still, it was this heightened perception that interfered with the reality of my lonely life years before.

I obtained internships my last two summers in college. After graduation, I secured a place in business school and took to heart every principle of business used by successful executives. My fascination with the career patterns that brought them to the top became the beacon that inspired every step I took moving forward. Even the relationship with Kena did not detract from my focus on the success I hoped to achieve.

Like all young men during their clean-sweat time, I gave no value to a grandmother's cold opinion of a beautiful woman with a perfect balance of physical parts. To Grandma's way of thinking, Kena put at risk all her work in molding and shaping me for my place in the world. "The whirling winds of manhood were blowing with hurricane force. No man can stand against them," was her spin on the relationship. Her only strategy was to keep alive her hope of a fuller life for me in another place beyond the limiting confines of life in Sero. But it was in another place that I began my relationship with Kena.

Because Grandma had never had a complete relationship with any man, even her own son, she could not see the many levels of a man. Even so, she knew by observation the power a young woman in the full bloom of her youth, had over a man. She could only wait and pray. In her eyes Kena was looking for a ticket to somewhere else and I was a First-Class fare.

The tragedy Grandma hoped never to see, finally unfolded. A baby was on the way. Her emotions left her. They were gone as if waiting with bags packed, ready to walk out the door without saying goodbye. Her hopes for me left to unlucky chance.

But her hopes rose again. Kena miscarried.

Years of professional responsibilities stole time from us, however our relationship held steady. Twelve years later, Deon was born.

11

From the beginning, the investigative reports were thorough. The original report identified Greg as the traitor, while at the same time he was smiling and knifing me in the back. The fact that he was from Mississippi, did not, at first, arouse any suspicions. He'd left the state as a young child. The final report revealed he still had relatives in Jackson, and to my horror, Sero. When I saw those words, I held my breath as a pricking sensation began to spread slowly through my body. Not moving, I read on. The Sero relatives lived about twenty miles from the nearest state road. The family name is Cady. The words swirled before me. Dumbfounded, I set paralyzed for almost an hour, my mind blank. Finally, the question forced itself, *Billy, what is your part in this?*

Once I regained my equilibrium, I decided the time had come to spring the trap and catch the snake. At that moment I could not bring myself to blame Billy for Greg's actions. My mind rejected any culpability on his part, I directed all my anger at Greg.

~

Wednesday morning, July 20th was another day of heat extremes. I chose a summer-weight classic dark blue suit:

one I wanted to project the executive power of a man not to be trifled with. The conservative look was standard. It could, however, play just as well for a funeral. But today another man's expensive suit, tie and shoes would be the ones remembered in the coming days and years. As usual my driver was on time to the minute. Despite the disquiet coursing through me, I held my face neutral. But something alerted him that this morning was different from all the others we'd shared. The inner storm must have shown in my eyes or the tense muscles of my neck.

I chose him from the pool because his direct manner in communicating reminded me of Grandma and Billy. Also, as with them, he and I had, on occasion, shared confidences and developed a high level of comfort with each other. He knew Billy's situation and the importance of my visits with him. He too, had a close relative serving time in prison. I could not, however, share with him Billy's probable connection to the problem in my office. Shame, hurt and anger would not permit it. I could barely breathe the thought myself.

The oppressive humidity raised the heat index an additional ten degrees. Even the shimmering haze looked weary. It cast a punishing glow over the rushing mass of humanity heading to cooler spaces. For a few hours, cubicles and offices, would give relief. Somewhere in the sea of vehicles, I knew there was another man also making the trip to the same modern skyscraper on the lower eastside. Because my thoughts were consumed by events that would take place in the coming hours, I took no particular notice of the obstacles of morning rush-hour. I remained cautious and watchful.

Not wanting the normalcy of my daily routine to appear out of place, I began our conversation talking about the weather and the latest antics of his favorite grandchild. He must have seen through the façade and spoke without ceremony. "I've chauffeured powerful men most of my working life and learned to read their emotions. I often recognize storm signals emanating from the back seat even when I cannot know the reason for them. There were times when the back-seater laid out the problem to me, unfiltered. Other times I'd been asked directly, what would I do under the specific circumstances presented. Then there were occasions when I had to find a place of solace for the back-seater: a discrete bar, a hotel room or the comfort of a woman whose place was familiar to me."

Mr. Joseph was a wise man, offering me options. Our eyes met in the rear view mirror. Few people could discern I was seething with emotions being held in check: the tight clenching of my jaws or the tell-tale muscles that periodically pulsed on each side of my neck. He knew. Through the mirror, I saw in his eyes a knowledge of people: that same knowledge I'd gained over the years reading other people's emotions. He continued, "Whatever trouble lies ahead, I am available to you anytime, night or day."

"You're right, there is trouble ahead." *Today someone will pay a high price for the turbulence of all the emotions you so aptly note.*

"I can't know the cost, but often I've heard about the price men paid, the strategies that worked and those that failed. For sure a life will change today."

That person was also driving to the same destination, protected from the heat only by the design of the pricey sports car that shouted the owner could be driven by someone else if he chose. I was sure he moved carefully through the teeming mass, not so much to protect the other travelers, but to avoid damaging his prized toy. Humility was not familiar to him. There was nothing cautious about his persona. His mantle announced financial success. He was sure of his place in the scheme of his life and he needed the world to know he'd made it. But like many young people, there is little or no room in his life for the possibility of changed circumstances. Success and the life it gave would last as long as necessary. I was sure, his vehicle, just as mine, inched carefully through the slow-moving traffic. Destiny lay in wait.

As I stepped from the car in the shadowed garage, my driver wished me a good day. I had no doubt about this day, "I will do everything to make it so."

My mind focused on the events which were to unfold shortly, taking down one man and possibly ruining the lives of other associates. I'd gathered close every strategy I ever used to get through a crisis: surviving the beating near the levee, holding my place in Grandma's house, and overcoming the often not so subtle racism on my rise to a vaulted place in this building. I'd even swallowed my pride after being passed over for a promotion given to the man I trained.

Entering the building, a kaleidoscope of images continued as I mentally stepped outside of myself recalling scenes from my childhood. Again, I saw a child abandoned and scared; then a boy, sometimes confused but always hopeful; and finally, the picture of a man, betrayed, but resolute. This is the man who stepped into the elevator as the door silently slid closed.

As I rode the elevator to my office, the mantle of survival tightened its grip. I slipped into the familiar nonthreatening persona. My thoughts turned to Deon. Being a father heightened my sensitivity to parenting ways, linking together my own experiences, especially my childhood fears of abandonment. These feelings don't go away, they just hide below the surface until some event, thought or word brings them rushing back.

The door opened noiselessly and contemplation of what lay ahead took full control of my mind. I emerged from the elevator ready for the maelstrom to come.

Still mentally observing myself, I relaxed my shoulders and pleasantly greeted my assistant as I entered our large suite. I did not allow myself to think beyond the moment. *In a few hours this will be over.* I needed to stand alert every second. The passing hours will take care of themselves.

"I put everything you'll need on your desk, no important calls today, should be a quiet day."

The responding smile that lit my face calmed me slightly. *You are way, way wrong,* but said instead, "We can use more of them."

An hour later, I still held my attention in a vise, focused only on the papers in front of me. Hour two came and passed. I was able to conduct business as I did every day even as people came in and out of my office. Hour three ticked away. I avoided any necessity that would take me from the floor. One more hour and all hell broke loose.

The sound started as a low buzz. It merged with the thumping noise in my head and my increased heartbeat, racing like a storm. From what seemed a far distance, I heard my assistant's anxious voice. "There is something going on down the hall."

With supreme effort, I asked, "What is it?' Before she answered, the noise grew louder. When I stepped into the hall, I saw one or two people gathered outside Greg's office. *So, it has begun.*

Out of the blue I remembered Billy's statement, "I endure in this place because my first and last thought everyday is survival. If you intend to hold your own in a white man's world your every thought had better be survival."

With purpose and the appearance of urgency, I walked down the hall. Before I said anything, the person in charge said, "This man is under arrest."

My eyes locked with Gregg's who was now handcuffed, hands behind his back. Intimate knowing passed between us. The calm demeanor he tried to project did not hold true. I saw through to the inner eye. In his enlarged pupils, I saw surprise, followed by fear, then revenge. Generations-old hatred caught fire in his eyes and burned freely. I made sure he saw, in my eyes, only the raw feelings I'd held so long: uninhibited anger. So that I would not falter, Grandma's ghostly voice reminded me, "Cut off the head of the venomous snake." Then Mr. Fitzgerald's parting advice, "The cost must be paid, you or him." Finally, Billy's voice chimed in, "It's your survival man."

For Greg only, my eyes spoke for me, *I know your traitorous actions.* The interaction lasted a millisecond, but each would forever remember the message.

"Sue call legal counsel to arrange bail."

Taking a calming breath, I moved to offer an explanation to the other employees who watched the drama play out in stunned silence. I promised to advise them when I had more information.

I didn't trust myself to draft a report immediately following the take down. I needed time to shed emotions that could be interpreted in any way, other than Greg's criminal involvement in matters that had nothing to do with the company. Once I had complete control of my emotions, I went to the house counsel, gave an oral narrative of the incident. Back at my desk I put the events, as I observed them, with the information from arresting officers in a formal report which I sent to legal counsel.

12

My burning need to immediately rush down to the prison nearly overwhelmed me. But my sense of survival demanded I remain in New York in case Greg drew me into his web of deceit. With Herculean effort, I worked to keep my emotions in check, however, the morning I snapped at my assistant, was the scariest day of my career. I was losing control.

One week after Greg's arrest, he was released under home confinement. The next day I was back at the prison, my emotions seesawing between deep hurt and anger. As Billy sat down on the other side of the bullet proof glass, my clenched jaws and unsmiling face told him immediately this visit would be different. I was back to confront him. Unlike our usual visits, this time I spoke first, accusing him. "What the hell are you trying to do to me?"

For a solid minute he said nothing. Then he raised his hands, palms up. "Listen to me. Please."

But I insisted, "How could you do this to me?"

"We only have a little time, listen." He rushed on, overly anxious to tell his story and in my heart, I hoped for a denial. But true to his nature, he made no apology, just jumped in, skipping the easy banter we usually shared at the beginning of our visits.

"You and I were mirror images of each other: two boys smarter than most, curious, even-tempered and most of all refusing to allow the social environment to stand as a barrier against the smooth flow of our daily lives. I took a wrong turn, thinking I was smart enough to win any game. I knew what my cousins down in Jackson were doing. If I could see their goings on, then surely the law would soon see what they were doing."

I did not respond to his pause in the story. Breathing hard, he gathered himself and continued. "My need to achieve at something burned like a house on fire. You were building your life as destiny demanded. Me, I was still stuck in a Sero life, finally realizing I was going nowhere at the speed of light. Their little enterprise was something I could put my mind to.

I proposed my assistance. When their shock wore off, I was in and immediately adjusted the way they were doing things. There were people in the group we had to get rid of. That wasn't easy, but I tightened the organization by making it a more family-run operation."

"What about me? I didn't want to hear a long explanation.

"Wait man, listen." He was breathing harder. "The next thing I did was study how these operations work. You'd be surprised the amount of information one can obtain just by studying media accounts and reports about the industry. We needed to operate way under the radar. I convinced the others it was necessary for me to participate with as little contact with them as possible. So, for the first four or five months I was involved, we went dark. I knew from my research we could move forward when we decided the time was right."

As he told the story I was perversely fascinated, but not surprised. He was a natural leader and always assumed others would follow his lead. His strength was in planning, strategizing and understanding how things work. Not able to stop myself, I asked, "How did you get rid of the people you wanted out of the operation?"

"We gave that operation to them and by going dark for a time, they didn't consider us competitors. Anyway, I had higher aspirations for us."

"So they just faded away?"

"No, we faded into the background while I restructured."

"That must have been a dicey time. People just don't give up drug territory. They claim it, own it and kill for it when necessary."

"Of course you're right on target. We left Jackson and moved the operation. A university town is always prime territory. We didn't forget about Jackson, but it was out of the picture for a time. The folks there were selling different products. My thought was that we should specialize in only one product. My research revealed we had more flexibility if we stuck with synthetic drugs. We could switch chemicals when necessary. We'd have more control."

And I know how you like control. "They just let you move in and assume the leadership?"

"My cousins were country boys who didn't exactly understand clearly how to conduct their lives outside of their closed way of living. We started small, buying by purchasing small amounts of the chemicals we needed and mixing them ourselves. We tried them out by giving test mixtures to people who were looking for a cheaper option. Man, you can't imagine the hunger for these drugs on college campuses. Our operation began to grow at a steady pace. These kids often need help in staying up nights, completing assignments.

I continued my research in establishing a supply chain. That part of the game was tricky because in order to make the operation profitable, we needed to bring in additional people who were not family members. So, I brought in some of your people. With little consideration, they are always so anxious to make quick money. But, the upside to those boys was their connections to networks across the state line into Memphis. A major leap forward for us."

"What was it about this enterprise that drew you so deeply?" I was being sucked into his story even as my anger set waiting to ask again, why me?

"I wanted to make something of myself. It was never going to happen in Sero. Unlike you, I had no options." He paused as if remembering the exact moment he made his momentous decision.

"It became clear to me you were only passing through our little corner. You were constantly asking questions: never satisfied. And then there was your Grandma Neetha. The way she raised you was not for Sero, but for someplace else."

"What do you mean?"

"The way she made you dress was one thing. When you went to school, everything you wore was pressed and your shoes were just right. It's hard to describe, but I thought you always looked smart. Even the clothes you wore for play were up a notch."

"Wow."

"Wait a minute, let me finish. She had rules for you man, rules. She cared about what was happening in your life."

"That's a fact."

He kept talking, seeming not to hear me, as if he were telling his story to someone else. "During school time you had to be in your house when darkness fell, at least in the yard. The only reason I wandered home when I did was because I had no one else to hang with, no place to go. I envied the caring you had. Do you ever remember my mother or anyone from the house calling or sending for me? Tell the truth, can you?"

He sounded sad and hopeful at the same time. I quickly searched my memory for some sign from those years that would refute his recall of a loveless childhood. I could not help him. In all our years together, his family never figured in his daily life. My strongest memory of his mom was of her sitting alone on the porch or sometimes with his sister. His father did odd jobs here and there, mostly out of town.

"Confirmation by silence. You must see I was compelled to find a way out. You had left and during your trips back, I saw clearly you were on a path to your destiny."

Again, he paused. I held my questions, not wanting to interfere with his flow, but still anxious to know how he dragged me into his scheme. For the first time in all our years together, he seemed to be working his way through the twists and turns of his life, maybe, just maybe with a few regrets.

"I even imagined Grandma Neetha cared about me. She never stopped me from coming to the house: inviting me to eat whenever I was on the scene."

That was to keep an eye on you when we were together.

"There were times after you went in, I set on the ground across the street staring at your house, imagining what was going on inside. You had a real life and I never stopped wanting one for myself."

"I didn't have any more of life than you did. We could eat, we went to school, had time to play; what else did we need?"

"I rest my case. All your needs were covered by Ms. Neetha, even your future. She had a plan for you to succeed in life. Look at you. You landed just at the point she envisioned, maybe exceeding her vision. Everyone knew you would take the big step one day. We were temporary points in your life."

Once again, he overwhelmed me with his explanation. "You never had any idea of just how temporary my life had been before Sero. When our adventures began, we were equals. Any betting man observing two boys: one white, the other black, would naturally put his money on the white boy. His transcendent rise was laid out for him. The black boy, on the other hand, had a gauntlet of obstacles to run just to stay alive. Nothing has changed."

"What really happened? The white boy raced to the gates of hell and swung them open entering with abandon. The black boy bided his time, careful with every step. The betting man was destined to lose every dime."

Did you ever consider what you were doing to me? "Why all the self-mutilation now?"

Again, he took a long, hard breath. "Its time. Anyway, I began to ingratiate myself into the lives of those privileged college kids. It was easy. They're high achievers who were big fish in their home ponds. They arrive on campus and are thrown into a bigger pond often with much bigger fish. With some, their doubts and fears begin to overtake them. I can spot them every time. They tend to operate on the edges, outside the center of a group, you know, followers. I offer a little something to boast their confidence."

"Just like that?"

"I didn't just walk up to a person and say, 'I have something for you.' I become friendly, go to their parties, smile as if I'm part of the college family. We gather at the popular hangouts. They don't know I'm not a student. Who talks about classwork when you're drinking and trying to pick up girls? That's when my little boosters are introduced. They're exotic, not the street drugs they've been warned to avoid. They're affordable and they help them to have a more pleasant experience during leisure time. It was not a hard business to cultivate. Friends told friends and the operation grew."

"How were you able to convince them you were a student?"

"I didn't need a sophisticated vocabulary to make a connection and blend in. Most of the kids weren't looking to test the validity of anyone before engaging in conversation. Surprisingly I enjoyed the college vibes and often pretended I was actually part of the student body. I engaged in a dark and dirty business, but there was still a part of me that remained separated from my daily activities. I saw a life that was possible if I walked away from my burgeoning business."

"You could have easily made it in college. School was always a snap for you."

"You never knew, but I didn't show up for my final exams. I didn't get a diploma."

"You're not making sense; you made top grades and had already earned your diploma." Even though we attended separate high schools, I knew of his disregard for school rules. He did his homework only if it pleased him. Whenever I questioned him about it, he would say, "I'll do it when I'm ready." It worked for him. His teachers accepted his work when he decided to complete the assignments. He could have taken the finals even after the due dates.

"How would my life be any different from one day to the next with a diploma? Think about it. You had a plan for your next step. Me, on the other hand, I had a mother who wore out more chairs on the front porch than I can count. My father came home every so often with just enough money to stave off starvation. Every chance I had, I ate with you and Ms. Neetha. On those days I didn't have to concern myself with the possibility of little food at home."

"You never even hinted." It must have been hard; the sharpness of his memories clashing with the forgotten meanings I had no attachment to. Grandma's voice chimed in. "He doesn't need your sympathy."

Our friendship was forged, not in crisis or domination of one over the other, but in the everyday give-and-take moments that over time bound us together with ties as strong as blood. He always lived life as it presented itself, so I was surprised to hear him describe the events and ideas he found important.

We looked hard at each other, forcing to the surface memories from a past that had little meaning to the present. Time had stolen from one and rewarded the other. In that moment together, we understood the power and reach of destiny. We didn't talk about any secret aspirations he may have had, yet his memories and obsessive recall of our youthful experiences are still so real to him.

"My need to have a relevant purpose for just existing was so strong I was willing to do anything. You were going forward in an important way; I tried to emulate the same process."

"They're not the same thing, I work for a global corporation. My business is legal."

"But it was obvious, you were top dog, the man in charge. I wanted that. When I began developing my network, I thought of myself as a young man on the way up the corporate ladder. I keenly observed the students, looking for additional clues. Those college kids have an attitude of entitlement; feel they deserve whatever they want from life. It was the same with you. Your school and your teachers led you to believe you were entitled to more in life.

Remember we would talk about what it meant for everybody to have the same rights. It was exotic talk. You went to one school, I went to another, both of us in school. What was different? Your teachers helped you look to the future. I cannot recall a single time I heard anyone of my teachers talk about opportunity or possibilities. But it seemed to be the theme at your school."

"True. At my school the teachers knew the past and the urgency for a different future. You didn't need to hear the constant drumbeat of a hard time ahead with preparation being the only method of survival. Yes, they did emphasize the need for careful planning. But It wasn't necessary for you to hear the exhortations for excellence. For you, the past was the future. History did the talking. What you would get from school was just a piece of paper showing you'd put in the required time."

"Still I envied you."

"No matter how close we are; I'll never understand that."

"Please, just listen and let me continue."

"Sure." Listening to him tell how he began a process that almost ruined my life, while at the same time trying to emulate it, was like altered reality. But I fell right back into our old ways, crediting his brilliance with the ability to take control of any situation he focused on.

"Another thing, those college students believed they lived above the users who had to steal to support their habits. Some had money from allowances and trust funds. When their money ran out, all they needed to do was ask for more and it was sent immediately. As long as that happened, they had no need to think of themselves as addicts. This was a business where you didn't need to chase your customers. They were happy to pay the price. It was so easy. Using the mail made us more efficient. College kids are always getting packages from home, so mail service became an integral part of the business."

"How did you expand your growing business?"

"As I told you, I'd studied how to make these compounds, therefore I was able, through the internet, to get the materials I needed from different places. If one type of chemical became unavailable or scarce, I could easily switch products and when necessary, suppliers. T.J. this was an easy business to operate."

"So easy it landed you in this place." Years ago, he'd provided a sketchy outline of his hellish descent into drug trafficking, but today he explained the story with passionate details. "How long were you in this so-called business?"

"Years. I expanded to campuses in Memphis and Nashville. I even developed a small presence in Jackson again."

I felt out-of-body. "At what point did you bring in Greg?"

"He was already in college, but I need to go back a little. Early on he exhibited all the signs of a bright child. He was personable and curious, so unlike the rest of the family. As time passed, he spoke about a future. He would say things like, 'I want to go here or to some other place; when I'm grown, I'm going to do this, or I want to see that place.' You could see his brain working. One of his older brothers was selling drugs on the streets of Jackson so he wasn't unfamiliar with the business. He was a natural. In time, I simply put it to him, 'Do you want to make some money?'

He didn't hesitate to join me, just at a distance. He too was testing himself. He is the younger half brother of the boy you and I caught with that girl by the dam. Our first few years together he became my confidant and we built a closed relationship where he learned about people and how their needs would literally trap them in our web."

"Why didn't he see illegal involvement in drugs would not lead him to a brighter future?"

"But he did see possibilities. He'd done well his first two years in college and was looking toward graduating and getting work in the corporate structure. He was learning how to read people and understand human nature. That is a powerful skill in any business. You can attest to that."

"Absolutely. Training always includes understanding your listener, opponent or buyer. In today's world, of course, it includes understanding the cultural references of people from other countries." Instantly I recalled Greg's disarming smile so like Billy's. The impression he made on me at our first meeting was that of a person without guile, holding back nothing. "At what point in your plan did you decide I should be drawn into the enterprise?" Once again, I felt outside myself as if I were an observer.

"It wasn't that I wanted to draw you in, you were the only person I knew working in a corporation. I learned about that process from you. I was fascinated and internalized every word you used describing your professional life. When he was in business school, I advised Greg to try as hard as possible to get into your company. You didn't know him because he never came to Sero. He was born to a woman his dad had outside the marriage. His mom's people had a vision for him to succeed. They pushed him."

"And their efforts paid off. He worked hard, made himself available at all times and was always a team player. Too bad he put all that at risk." I forced the issue again, "Why me? Why did you push him on me, to sabotage my life?"

"I wanted to test your balls man. Old game."

Shock took hold of me leaving hurt to limp after it. I had no comeback, so I closed off any response. His tone and the way he picked his words, describing his decent into hell, against my will, intrigued me. I still needed to hear every detail of the road that took him so far from the possibilities that were his if only he'd reached out and grabbed them.

"We have a little time left and I feel I must tell you everything." He rushed to continue his explanation seeing the angry look return to my face.

"And I need to hear it all." I felt cold, even as I struggled to find any reason to hold him blameless for Greg's actions.

Billy neither wavered nor flinched, just continued his tale. "I decided it was prudent to have as little contact with my cousin as possible. While in college he pretended to befriend fellow students and made referrals when the time was right, not participating in any drug use himself. He'd tell them that he'd heard so-and-so could put them in touch with someone who had access to what they wanted. That is how he started, easy as eating pie.

He enjoyed it. The thrill of outsmarting others was a powerful motivator for him too. He developed a competitive way of thinking. Neither of us was totally motivated by money. It was like playing a sophisticated board game; move and countermove. He was in it for the long haul. One thing led to another and I encouraged him to get internships so he could see first-hand how things in corporations worked. As you noted he was a quick learner, the kind of young man any company clamors to bring on board."

I nearly gasped. How did I miss this corner of Billy? I knew his brilliance. There were no stop signs in his life. He decided things for himself. And that was a powerfully seductive idea for a boy like me who, even in my teens, still feared the possibility of being sent away from the only home I knew.

Billy began to speak again, conjuring up the picture of a mentor guiding his mentee in the ways of successful upward movement. "I became his life coach. My focus became getting him into your company and have him rise like a soaring wind or eagle, something like that. Anyway, I trained him to always size up a prospect, from a distance of course. There could be no connection between us."

A loudspeaker announced the end of visiting time. I stood immediately with a strong need to square my shoulders against my whole existence being ripped apart. After walking a few steps toward the exit, I turned and he was still sitting, watching me.

"We'll continue this discussion next time."

"I'll see you then," he smiled sadly.

13

Two weeks later I walked into the dull gray building still hoping to hear Billy express regrets about facilitating Greg's direct path to my office. I refused to accept his explanation that just by keeping abreast of my professional moves, he could guide Greg to a position in the company and ultimately into my department.

He looked different; his chalk-white face more drawn and his eyes opaque, no longer clear gray. I noticed when he entered the room, he seemed to shuffle. But his smile was unchanged. Eager to resume his story he began at the exact point in our conversation where he'd left off at the end of the last visit.

"Let's go way back." After a coughing fit, he began again, "Greg's father took him away. His father had an idea that somehow they could do better away from Mississippi. They went first to live with his dad's parents outside of Pittsburg."

"I'm stunned I never connected him to your family. All this time you were able to hide the trail of a scheme that could end everything I worked to achieve."

"If you remember, I continued to tell you to examine everyone in your life. Think about it. When you were here in June, I told you to let your investigation include people close to home. And what did you do, you thought I meant looking at your relatives. I still see Sero as our home, however, it has a different connotation for you."

"Yes, you did."

"You never saw Greg. He was a skinny kid dominated by his half brother, Peter who married that girl you caught him with. They had some kids they couldn't care for, eventually she began to drink heavily, and they drifted in different directions. Even I can't describe how much he hated you."

"For seeing a naked white girl?"

"You should have known his anger and hatred directed at you would not go away. Even though you left Sero, word got around about your successes. As you moved higher, Peter sank lower."

"That doesn't make sense."

"Most of what happens in life, doesn't make sense. Luck of the draw determines our outcomes."

"If I believed that, I'd still be living in Sero or someplace just like it."

"Maybe, maybe not. Your grandma wouldn't have it."

"She had a lesson for every one of life's turns and her every thought was that I would go out into the world, enter the struggle and make my way. She would ask me, 'What is it you want to see happen?' The question never varied. I had to have an answer she would accept."

"That is exactly what Greg's mother's family wanted for him. They stoked hope in him and pushed him hard; college, business school, the works. His dad knew our side of the family did not understand possibilities. One day he took Greg and walked away. By then, though, Greg was already attached to his older brother, Peter, so his dad allowed visits between them for a time. He stoked his anger against you for seeing that naked girl all those years before. That hatred was the only tangible thing in his life. He kept it alive and at every opportunity, passed it on to Greg before contact between them ceased."

"How did he connect with me?"

"I made the connection. You were the only one who ever left Sero, but you carried your footprints, leaving none behind for others to follow, except me. When you left for college, I never let those footprints out of my sight. Whenever they began to fade, stories of your success sharpened my focus. Greg was able to get into your company and then onto your team. This was a new wind blowing his family's way and they savored his success."

"And because he demonstrated such a strong work ethic, I put more and more responsibility on him. He shouldered it well, embracing the company like a family."

"His actions were no different in our operations. In college when he came upon a person he considered a good prospect, he brought him into the foal by referring him to our people. It was second nature to him. Our team was just as efficient as your team."

Then how were you caught? My eye contact with him never waivered.

"I can read your thoughts." Billy's ragged smile never faltered, as he continued, "There is always the risk of losing control with increasing expansion of a business. You understand that."

"Yes, it's a very important aspect of business. What was it about him that we missed, some aspect of his personality that he could immerse himself in a dual life so completely?"

"I pitched family loyalty to him."

"How would you know about family loyalty?"

Billy paused. The look on his face was no different than that of an eager department head inspiring a team member. "I didn't need to put pressure on him. His parents had drummed the importance of family support into him so strongly, that when I approached him, he never stopped to think about where it would lead."

"Surely it would not lead him to the life his parents envisioned."

"He was already on the road to a better life when I invited him to join us."

"Where did he expect it to lead?" I was still looking for any hint of remorse.

"Maybe to replace you."

"How could you know his deepest motives?"

Billy looked at me with disbelieving eyes. Once again, his voice took the tone of father to son, "Blood."

The quiet pause between us thickened. "T.J. have you forgotten? There was nothing I enjoyed better than observing other people and discerning the reasons behind their actions. Greg was easy prey. Now you realize the intensity of the grudge they held against you for seeing that skinny bitch without a stitch on.

Greg learned all he could through internships he acquired. When he finally landed at your company, I directed him to make his way to a division or department directly in your sight and work like his life depended on it."

"And he did. He seamlessly integrated himself into the department. It is surprising he could perform at the level he did and still be involved in your activities."

"Don't forget we had no personal contact after the initial set-up. Our system included encouraging messages from me through his family. Things like 'the more you achieve, the higher we all rise,' meant something special to him but nothing to anyone reading it. These messages were meant to push him harder, so he'd become indispensable to his colleagues."

"Everyone found him easy to work with. Because he worked so hard, it wasn't necessary to push the other members of his team. He made himself look like a special kind of leader."

"A leader like you."

"That's probably why I noticed him. He exhibited all the skills I'd been trained to use. He set himself up to be noticed, making his colleagues comfortable, while keeping the edge on his competitiveness."

"Bet you didn't know, he paid for short training courses himself, beyond those offered by the company. No one knew, he attended on his own time."

Even as I set listening to Billy's narrative of an all-out attack on my life that was a mere game to him, I experienced creepy feelings of our old camaraderie. I was perversely impressed. As kids we'd always played mind games with each other. He'd raised the ante and developed a single-minded focus on building a successful illegal enterprise. This ruthless Billy established a tight team enforcing compliance with consequences supplied by associates. His venture proved to be solid with unlimited customers. He could have gone all the way to the top of any legitimate venture he chose.

"Why did Greg stick with your plan for his life: a plan which could destroy me? He was living on his own, away from his family; breaking from your schemes would not have been a problem."

"I didn't put forth a plan to harm you, just as I said, I'd reached a point in my mind where it was important to test my limits. I was anxious to be as good and powerful as you. It made my life more bearable.

Every fiber of my being stood at attention. I fought off the painful hurt as his words came like missiles. This, of course, was the Billy I knew. And I was collateral damage.

"You obviously were able to finally break free of Sero. Did you ever consider expanding your education and moving on from that point?"

"Why did I turn left when I could have turned right?"

"Yes."

"To be honest, I don't know. The thing is, I began feeling a sense of anticipation the minute I started playing with the idea of breaking society's rules. It was as if I'd been waiting for this opportunity all my life. I threw myself into the game without any reservations. It was exciting man even if dangerous. As I said, it gave my life a plan."

I could feel myself beginning to ask again, why, but this explanation fit his personality. It seemed so familiar, as in childhood when we would sit together and scheme about small things. His mind worked the same as he described his decent into a dark and illegal world where the only reward for winning, was the destruction of lives.

"I understand the excitement of winning. My entire professional life is about winning. Ultimately I won this game by tracking Greg who was a mere pawn in your game." *And so were you*, Grandma's voice echoed from the grave.

"Then you get it." His crooked grin widened, revealing as much excitement as the dismal surroundings permitted.

With him sitting in front of me, telling his incredible story of attacking my life, I forced myself to admit, I'd ignored all the signs of his insecurities. His neediness was clearly evident. I'd also consciously decided to be colorblind about him. From our early days his friendship was more valuable to me than the natural lines that would have divided us. The decisions I made about him then were important to me, as they are still. How was it he couldn't exercise the power that was his birthright. Struggle, for him, would have been almost nonexistent.

My mind returned to the conversation and his explanation of Greg becoming a valuable member of my team, even as he became an integral part of Billy's scheme. "My life became a game?"

"But you understand the excitement of the hunt, the scent of being close to the prey, finally succeeding. Anyway, I decided we would look into using overseas possibilities."

"Was that before or after you knew my company had Chinese connections?" I was so hurt; I didn't consider the logic behind my question. He seemed to be proud of his twisted path.

"One of the things I always emphasized was for him to be on the lookout for any opportunity. I'm not sure he saw this as an opportunity, but I did. Cultivate friendships with those you meet in your professional life, I advised him. Don't push, just be friendly and appear to be accommodating. At some point your path will cross that of someone who considers you a foolish American. In their eyes, we're saps, easy prey. When that happens, go with the flow. Eventually you'll form a link with the person that may lead to other opportunities."

"You were also putting his life on the line. What if he'd been caught?" Fear of his answer prevented me from asking, *or me?*

"He needed to be tough. This is not a world for squeamish people."

"How would you know?"

"You're a brilliant man, you must know my everyday existence is a jungle fight for survival even before I was put under lockdown."

For a second the room's temperature spiked as I instantly recalled so many of the details of his complicated scheme. He'd worked briefly in Arkansas as an assistant field representative with a hospital association. He said that gave him the opportunity to study the basic movement of drugs through the health system. It was his way, to understand more about the business he intended to exploit. It was important to know how patients in pain respond to drugs. He studied the effects of different drugs on the brain. He knew which drugs excited, which drugs calmed patients and which drugs gave a feeling of power. No detail was too small.

He read accounts of drug busts and saw how stupid people were making stupid decisions that led them straight to jail cells. They bought fancy and expensive cars and flashed big money on every scene.

His words stuck in my mind. "The idea of being an unseen hand behind the largest money-making game available, intrigued me. My appetite for that kind of power could only be satisfied according to rules I designed, building the group, person by person based on their loyalty. It was not a huge group. I started small, perfecting the mission using only one member of my family to keep notes on every aspect of the business. Once the operation was set up I had very little contact with the frontline people. In most criminal operations like this, the top man keeps his hands on the money. For me, however, money was not my first priority. Managing a successful business scheme invigorated me.

By learning every aspect, I was able to spot weaknesses and opportunities. The burgeoning synthetic drug market offered the greatest opportunity. I zeroed in on it and saw my opportunity in assembling the chemicals needed for manufacture. Then I began an intense study of these chemicals, learning what steps needed to be taken so synthetic chemicals could be substituted for the natural ones. I made my team a significant cog in the networks that were already in place."

During all those hours I set on a hard metal seat, listening to his narrative, I had the unreal sensation that we were back sitting under the big tree in Grandma's backyard or hanging out down by the levee. He never told me what he did with his illicit money. Holding that information was another exercise of power. I don't believe the authorities knew the full extent of his part in providing raw materials for the drugs and their movement onto the next stage of the process.

The intensity of my anger could only subside when my hurt, that came in bitter waves, had answers. Why? Was it his intention to halt my career? How could he do this to me? I couldn't satisfy myself he would intentionally attack me with such a cunning plan, even though I heard it, word for word directly from his mouth. What was his true purpose? These questions would not go away. They'd found a comfortable home in my soul and there they burned ferociously.

~

I'd made no plan to stop in Sero after the visit. With more than a three-hour wait once I reached the airport, I found a quiet corner, hid myself in an empty booth and gave free reign to the tumultuous war raging in my mind.

The day I learned of his arrest I immediately went to visit him. At first, I didn't allow myself to believe he was guilty, however, I wanted him to know that our friendship remained undiminished. During that first visit we never discussed his plight, instead we reminisced about happier times. He appeared incredibly relaxed for a person facing forever in jail. How does a free spirit adjust? During the years, I noted subtle changes; loss of color being the most prominent. Even in the mean circumstances of his confinement, he maintained an understated measure of leadership. He was often allowed extra visitation time. I noticed other prisoners deferred to him. Making peace with his situation was a constant part of his daily existence.

A distance of more than a thousand miles separated us, yet he was able to form a plot that could take away my hard-earned dignity. Even as I hoped for an expression of regret, I continued to feel I couldn't exist without him, my first friend, my brother. I was always able to depend on him. Memories of that awful night when he rescued me from death blows flooded my senses as they had done so many times before. *He saved my life.*

Out of nowhere Grandma's voice came to life. "Billy, just like every person in this life, has to pay his dues. Some people pay early, others later. Even the man who thinks he's done everything to escape the dues-paying is surprised when the moment arrives and one of life's circumstances knocks on his door and demands payment. For him the paying may be forever. It is so with Billy."

But this isn't about dues-paying.

"What then?" The voice wouldn't stop. "A special friendship as you keep describing it? A stab in the back maybe?" I refuse to let this situation take away our long history. His life took a wrong turn: maybe he really didn't have a way out of Sero.

She joined the internal argument again, "His way out was never in question. He was born with his feet pointed toward the exit."

You never understood Grandma.

"I understood your conflict. You needed attachments in your life. Billy Cady was fine for a time, but I hoped when you left for college his friendship would no longer be something you relied on."

I did rely on it, friends are friends. You don't abandon someone because new people come into your life. He saved my life Grandma. Those boys almost beat me to death. I'm alive because of him.

"No, the beating was because of him. Had you not been running with him, you would never have encountered that piece of trash."

I quieted the argument for seconds, but the self-talk would not let go. A creeping feeling of shame began to wash over me. I fought back. Still the ghostly voice of Grandma throttled on. "God gave you life, the life of a man; then He heaped on the life of a black man. Your need for survival began at that moment and it continues, no matter how you try to set it aside. You can't out-run survival. Make it your friend."

I have a right to pause and take a short break, to step away from survival's grip.

"No pause. No break."

You lived in a different world.

"Same world."

Shaking my head in denial, but to no avail, the voice continued.

"You never needed Billy's approval. You became a distraction to him, a boy who was destined, by circumstance, to drift through life. He was needy."

So was I Grandma.

A hushed silence settled over me as I tamped down the doubtful thoughts that, if continued, would separate me from a relationship that helped me through the rocky times of my youth. Even now, knowing his betrayal, I'm grateful. But why did he put my life in jeopardy? I can't accept he was trying to hurt me. How would that benefit him? He is my best friend.

The ghostly voice kicked in one more time. "A friend will never stab you in the back and then stand on your bloody body."

Why are you trying to take someone I value from me?

"His value ran its course long ago, move on."

Grandma, please.

"Let go."

Impossible, I still live by much of life's lessons I learned through my times with him. To let go would be to drain away half my life.

Her voice sneaked back. "The lesson that saved you was the one that led you away from Sero. That is not a path you can attribute to him. Lessons from the failures of your family that I kept alive, were more valuable than any talk from someone who came from nothing."

You never let that go. True, his family history was just as pitiful as mine, but he had potential.

"Potential beckons a person forward. It's only real work that moves him ahead."

There are no arguments against that. You pushed me. No one was behind Billy to push him. That was his downfall, the reason his choices led him to a jail cell.

14

The trip left me with inner turmoil rippling like water in a boiling cauldron that could not find its way to the surface, but still churned with deadly force. Back in the office I made myself busier than ever, trying to prevent intrusive thoughts overtaking me during times of quiet. For several days I stayed with Rita, hoping to soothe my hurt. It seemed to work. Just as with Kena, she allowed me emotional space, making no demands. By the end of the week I remained troubled: restless sleep, tossing and turning, while gripping her tightly. In the quiet hour before dawn I finally fell into deep sleep impervious to sounds, words and the dreaded thoughts of Greg's treachery that continued to disturb my longing for peace. Hours later, after these demons quieted themselves, I opened my eyes, calling Rita.

She came with a hot cup of coffee and slipped back into bed. This was truly a rare occasion for me. Rising early and getting on with things is how I usually begin each day. But today I hesitated, needing a diversion from increasing thoughts that demanded I accept Billy's own words and explanations, or reject all we'd been to each other most of our lives. *He is just as much my family as Grandma.*

"What's on your mind?" Even though I held her close, she sensed my thoughts resided in another place.

"Billy,"

Unchecked, a shocked expression crossed her face. I'd been distracted since returning. Usually my only distractions were Deon or my work. My continued help in Billy's difficult circumstances was set; putting money into his prison account, sending sneakers, accepting all those calls and the visits. I made no changes.

"Is there a problem?" She questioned me further after I shook my head. "What then?"

"Right now, I think I'll put Billy in the corner," holding her even tighter, putting an end to further talk, I pressed my lips gently to hers. Once again, the haunting image of that white body standing by the levee, so strange, yet so enticingly beautiful, flashed through my mind. Shutting out the image, my body, urgently, moved against the flesh and blood woman I held in my arms. Taking her with a violent stroke of lust mixed with misunderstood vengeance, anger and other emotions I had no words for, gave me pleasure, but no peace. Soothing her after my explosive release did little to calm the swirl of vivid images of white marble flesh filling my head. Buried deep in my psyche, the decades-old image never left me.

Reigning in the fragmented thoughts, I watched her sleeping. *I owe you.* Gently, peeling back the sheet and running my fingers softly along her thigh, I admired her golden color. *Such a contrast with Kena's creamy brown skin.*

"I'm yours for the remainder of the day, Let's not waste it." I whispered in her ear even though there was nothing in the room to disturb the quiet.

After a long stretch she opened her eyes with a smile that melted my heart. "What do you have in mind?"

"Anything you want."

"You sure?" She never pushed, allowing me to initiate our activities.

Needing her warm touch, I was reluctant to leave the bed. Another long kiss and the powerful shower spray eased the deep tension in my neck muscles. She joined me and once again I couldn't keep my hands from her. "You're sure we need to go out? I'm having fun here," she asked with a playful pinch of my buttocks, then pressed herself full length. "There is a much more pleasant way to spend the next few hours."

We spent the day in and out of vintage shops, buying nothing, then shared a light meal. For a while I was contented, needing our time together. Her place in my life is solid and I don't want her to feel neglected, but settling all my conflicting thoughts needed priority tonight. By eight o'clock I'd returned to my apartment.

Sitting on the sofa with my eyes closed, again I asked myself, what did I miss all these years? Friends trust each other. They help and rely on each other. All I could remember at the moment were the endless discussions Billy and I had daily. While I was preparing myself to rise to the next level, he was along for the ride. We identified with each other's habits. Neither judged the other. I thought both of us believed at the deepest level each could go as far as the distant horizon. Apparently, he measured his horizon through my journey. There is no doubt Sero offered zero directions to its young people, never teaching them to access a different future than the one that sat static for generations. I escaped because Grandma built a road for me, mile by mile.

My anger churned. I'd shared all my conflicting struggles about Kena and Rita with him, nothing hidden. He knew the secret hurt I carry to this day of my mother's abandonment. Billy couldn't possibly envy my life. My road just wasn't one he could travel, likewise I couldn't move on his, but in Sero the rules were murky. When we were growing up each of us knew white and black walked separate paths, so we didn't dwell on these different ways we were expected to always behave. Who cared? He was my best friend. We even strategized on what I could do if my mother tried to take me from Grandma's home. I didn't know at the time Grandma had her own plan, a real plan, not the flimsy hope of a young child.

~

Trust has always been a precious, but elusive commodity for me. At times its value flickers to life with my expectations, then fades with the intrusion of doubt and uncertainty. I struggle anyway. How can I trust the relationship I have with Rita? Am I just playing house with her? What does she really expect? Will she leave me if I don't promise more? Will Kena continue to accept only a part of me as she appears to? Which one of them will always stand with me?

Again, sleep eluded me, I decided to follow the thread of these competing thoughts and images, but I became more anxious with a continuing mixture of anger and loss hope. Always hovering in the background is my mom. At any time, even today, just thinking of her has the power to disrupt the balance of my life. Filling more and more moments dwelling on fantasy possibilities of what my life may have been with her, I sometimes mentally construct a separate universe from the one I had with Grandma. I pose questions as if she were still alive. The times you came back into my life were few and I remember each one of them with complete clarity. I struggle to recall hugs. Why weren't you interested in reuniting with me? Even after my decision not to leave with you, I hoped you would express some interest in taking me. There was the possibility you may have settled down to make a home for us. What would that have been like, a room of my own, maybe growing up with more than one friend, a place where relatives visited us, seeing your beautiful face every day? I imagine your touch and smile. I can only use my imagination as it was impossible to have a realistic remembrance. But I can never forget your electric looks: brown eyes so clear I thought there were no others like them. Your lips and that red lipstick you always wore framed a heart stopping smile, I can envision to this very day. Most of all, your lovely hair, thick and just the right length that you could wear in any style. The imagined sound of your voice when you call me to dinner or your tone when you ask about my school day; would you question me with a smile? Would you worry about my safety when I reached my teens? When I think about all of these possibilities, I wonder who else would you have let into our lives; a second chance for my father maybe.

Will these same questions visit my child years from now? Will he wonder about my commitment to him? Am I spending enough time with him? I talk to him almost everyday and visit as often as I can. Does he mention me to his teachers and friends? How does he answer when asked why his dad does not live with him?

My attempts to compare my childhood with Deon's only creates more uncertainty. He can point to many things: books, toys and souvenirs from around the world, that I bring to him. Would gifts have been sufficient for me to be assured of my mother's love and caring? There is no way I can have an honest answer. Sometimes a gift is evidence of love, at other times it only maintains a connection of ownership. What does a child own in his relationship with a parent? As a child Grandma owned nothing, not even her right to dream. Billy owned only the right to go wherever, whenever he pleased. I sure didn't own much. If the question were put to my child, what would he say?

Hours slipped by and the turmoil I felt before going to bed continued. Questions without answers held their ground, demanding responses. I went to the desk drawer and pulled out the final letter from Grandma and began reading it again. The edges were tattered, I'd read it so many times.

Dear Son,

I'm not long for this world so I decided to let everything out. These are my last words to you even as my heart beats to an uneven rhythm. With you I tried to make a man different from all the ones I knew. Sometimes it was a clash between God and me. Mostly, I saw only my own creation. How could I think my way was better than His? I think we ended in a draw, though now I can't be sure. But I still have something more to say, so bear with me.

The house is yours to do with it as you please.

Just remember it was more than a roof over our heads, it was a place of safety, comfort and joyous triumphs: your high school graduation and the mortgage payoff. It provided us a place to dream. When you left here you took not only your dreams, but in your pocket, you also carried my hopes that were sometimes hidden so deeply they shocked me when they dared to emerge. Like everything we carry around, the weight of a dream may become a burden. Then we put it into a closet hoping to protect it from the ravages of neglect and decay. When we leave it too long in the dark closet, like old clothes, the bugs and other creatures eat away at it. At first there are tiny holes we cannot see, and then we open the door to retrieve our hopes, only to find them in tatters.

I beg you, keep those dreams we made in your wallet and you won't be able to forget about them. Promise me.

That is my fight everyday Grandma.

I'm not sure you were always aware of my deep commitment to you, but you eventually stole my heart. I saw your struggles, courage, and when you could not hide them, your fears. Particularly, I paid attention to that Billy. I heard some of your conversations and observed the interaction between you two. I saw you holding your own, as the saying goes. But my heart almost stopped when Billy dragged you home that night, beaten to a pulp. I had to remain calm. There was nothing I could do to avenge the violence against you. Anything I did would bring the wrath of that no-good bunch of trash down on us. We would have to run. I just couldn't do it again. Please forgive me. But that incident made me more determined than ever to get you through high school and out of Sero. Your unreal comfort living with the ambiguous behavior of people in this town could weaken you for the tough ways of the world.

You would so often use the phrase, 'when I grow up'. I liked that part of you. Planning by the men in my family was something I hadn't seen. They were stuck where they stood, but you sensed a path in front of you. Thank God.

Make this little house work for you. It is a symbol of what a person can do who keeps going no matter the pain and there is plenty in life. If you don't know this pain yet, you will.

I'm jumping around; I just need to put my thoughts in writing. Sometimes I can speak my mind better this way. Being a person who had no safety expressing herself, I learned to keep all my thoughts and feelings hidden. But, my love for you never wavered.

I even consulted Mr. W.B. on how I could fight your mother if she came back to take you from me. As it turned out, I needn't have bothered. As the years passed, she became less and less of a threat. You were older and had some say-so.

All my other earthly belongings are yours to do with as you will. I have faith you will take care to make the best of everything. Don't worry about me.

Somehow, through the grace of God, I managed to survive. Imagine a country girl with no prospects, is able to lift herself higher, buying a place where she had the only key and actually having a decent life beyond anyone's expectations. I never invited my family from Alabama to visit. I was never sure whether they still owned the power to burst my bubble.

After coming to Sero, I concentrated on restarting my life piece-by-piece. I began every day with the clear knowledge that I had to make a go of things here. The return road home had no welcome back sign and Ohio was not a place I could settle myself. Sero was made for someone like me who only wanted to work hard and be left alone. Initially this was a place I could sit in my rented room and contemplate what might lie in front of me. I never had that opportunity before. Being the lifter of other people's burdens, kept me too busy to know I should have the burdens every woman was entitled to; what little affection from her man a black woman could expect and to sit on her porch watching the sun go down after putting her white woman's house in order. But most of all, to anticipate her man's needs so that he could meet his world the next day. I was in no position to figure out how I would get your grandfather here. Those imaginary thoughts I could only have after I came to Sero. Of course they were merely fanciful because as I knew him, he was satisfied with only what he could see in front of him and sometimes to his right or left. Years passed and eventually all hopeful thoughts of him were put away, locked inside a place we keep things to be eventually thrown away.

Even though I came prepared to work as hard as I ever did, I also knew that life hadn't promised me any reward or prize. The woman who rented me a room gave me information about people in the town and sometimes about those who had left. They didn't come back in summer to visit like they did back home. Those who had tried to make it here and did not, were gone for good. There was no growth in the population except for those children unlucky enough to be born here. The first weeks after I arrived, I tried to keep to myself: hard to do in a dusty dot just off a back road. But the church people never accepted my attempts at privacy. I joined the women's ministry and to my surprise, found it enjoyable. I felt I belonged. By the time you arrived I was a loyal member.

In a few months my life had changed like an explosive missile sending me on this strange journey. That is what life does for people like you and me. I always told you that we must do more than make the best of it. We must prepare for the next explosion, again and again. You prepared with as much protection as this life gives. Your education provides a measure of protection, however, there will never be enough education and experience that will allow you to let your guard down one minute. Consider this advice every morning you open your eyes.

Everything you have learned, you must tell little Deon. He's living a blessed life, but there are deadly explosions waiting for him just as they laid in wait for me, for you and so many before us. These lessons will add to his protection. Talk to him.

I know you'll be coming this way soon. Nothing has changed here. Our dusty roads still lead nowhere. But for me, the safety I felt when I first came, continues to comfort me. I am able to get a ride to the doctor's office when I need to. He tells me to continue doing what I'm doing and I'll be okay.

Finally, being able to retire I have nothing to do but clean the house. My knees ache almost continuously, but I can still work in my garden. I even made some new covers for your bed, spruced the room up a bit. I think you'll like it.

Through the Grace of God, I will still be here when you come home for your next visit. But if not, you have my parting thoughts in black and white.

One more thing, I was always reluctant to speak of it, but you have a right to know. Here it is. Your father may not have been your real father. Years after you came to live with me, he told me he wasn't sure. He said your mother had been close to another man before him. I didn't give it any credence. There was no way to tell. Why did he keep quiet so many years? Even though he was my own, I just concluded it was a statement men make when they want out of obligations. You should know.

Grandma

I did make it home just before she passed away. To know she was thinking of me near the end eased my sorrow. I learned from her friend Ms. Harry, who always accompanied her to the doctor, that she was sicker than she let on.

Her gravesite will be taken care of with the generous sum I gave to the church. I gave her remaining treasures to her few friends still living. All of my personal things had been removed years earlier. Only I will ever be able to tell the story of those important years together.

Grandma talked to me about so many things. Often the meaning of her words registered long after she said them; however, I don't think I ever got over my fear that I could lose my place in the home. I believed she loved me, but with conditions. It defines love for me no matter my attempts to think differently. What is the condition I place on my relationship with Kena? Why is she not enough? What does Rita give me that Kena cannot? Because I respect each woman's independent right to reject or accept me, I feel no need to take on feelings of guilt, so I leave the responsibility of acceptance to each, not pitting one against the other.

15

How ironic, in 21st century Mississippi, I can be next of kin to a dead white man. I stared out the window, not seeing the skyline below, just a scene of two boys sitting on a disintegrating levee, bantering back and forth about nothing of consequence. It was a recurring scene we shared more times than I can ever remember.

You were my first friend Billy Cady, my brother.

Even after his devastating revelations, I had one more visit with him. There was no way to know it would be our last. I should have recognized the signs. The constant coughing and hard breathing were definite clues he suffered serious health problems. His questions to me were more pointed. "You ever wonder why we don't match our hopes and dreams with how we live our lives?"

"Many times."

"Would you agree you've settled the conflicts of your early years?"

"No. I've learned to live with certain conflicts I can't settle."

"Like two women?"

"I don't know if that's an unresolved issue."

"Be honest now," he would not let go.

During every visit he asked about Kena and Rita. "When are you going to choose? Make up your mind, one of them has to be the front runner or maybe you can keep both of them?" He ignored my laugh and continued, "Seriously, who says a man can have only one woman?"

"Mostly society."

"Bullshit. Each woman brings her unique joy into a man's life. Think about it. Kena ties together your past and future. The connection is your son. On the other hand, Rita represents your present status. With her you don't need to remember past hurts, rough lessons and those corners of your life you want to forget. She's the one who soothes the day-to- day scrapes."

He sounded so rational, so eloquent, like a man with much experience. I knew there had been women in his life, but they seemed to have been fleeting relationships.

"East coast woman, west coast girl," he continued.

"It isn't that simple."

"Only because you've made it complex. You feel you owe Kena and that conflicts with your ability to let yourself fly free with Rita. Let the relationship take you wherever it leads. Leave the guilt trip behind, man."

"It's true. I want more from our relationship. I've been playing with the idea of having her move in with me."

"Go for it. Life is short. One day gone and another not promised."

Later as I thought back to his questions, I wondered if he was right? Am I being honest? Why can't I go any further with Kena? She's a woman to enhance any man's life.

Right up to the end he was still interjecting himself into my life and passing his final days dispensing brotherly advice. I wanted to know about those nebulous women who passed through his life, so I asked, "Was there a particular woman you thought about establishing a permanent relationship with?"

"A smile of remembrance briefly crossed his face, "There were a couple."

"What happened?"

"Detours happened. Like you, there were two women I had deep feelings for, but unlike you I was not conflicted about my feelings for them. There was a girl down in Jackson who first stole my heart. She was beautiful with a thick head of curly hair. I remember her being joyful, always smiling. It was a powerful attraction for me. My only real experience with women stemmed from my mother and sister, watching how they presented their hopeless lives: no independence, no expectation of anything better than the miserable muck of their days. You know that."

"Why couldn't you move forward with the Jackson girl?"

A sad quiet descended on him. "She had other plans for herself. She was a college girl." Seeing the shock on my face, he hastened to finish. "I met her in a fast food joint when she boldly came to me and asked if I mind sharing the table. She was seating herself even before I found my voice. She was just so beautiful, big black eyes that looked directly into mine. Her playful nature excited me in every way. You get my meaning. At first I thought it was a pick-up."

"What led you to conclude it was more?'

"Well, we set around long after our food was gone and when we separated, I had her phone number and a date. She and her roommate lived near a college. I learned she hadn't had too many dates before me. That was a surprise. A girl with her looks had to be in demand. I eventually learned she was a picky person."

"And she picked you?"

"I always behaved like a gentleman and my looks weren't so bad, well, not in those days. We had great fun together. With her I began to look at my situation differently, you know, seeing different possibilities. I dared to even think about college for myself. No one had ever talked to me about college. All I knew about it, I learned from you.

On our dates we went places I'd never heard of, mostly events on her campus. She was popular, with many friends. She was proud of me around them. That too was something I'd never experienced. You know how things were, I was totally ignored by my family, left on my own. I came and went as I pleased. With this girl I felt a definite responsibility to make her proud."

As he talked, I recalled a vague memory of a girl he mentioned once shortly after his arrest. "You know every detail of my life, but I never knew of this woman's importance to you."

"To this day I often think about her and what her life must be like."

"Why didn't this relationship go further?"

"Because she was a full-time student and I was working, as you know, in another venue, but we dated for several months. The most time we had together was on the weekends and we packed everything we had into those times together. It was great. Then one day I went to her apartment and her roommate said she had to go home unexpectedly. I didn't attach anything significant to it. My life had taught me to go with the flow. I just assumed she didn't have time to call me. T.J., a whole week went by without a word. Same thing the next weekend. I even sneaked by her place a couple of nights to see if she was there but avoiding me. Her roommate was not forthcoming with any information. She claimed this was the first year they'd roomed together, and she didn't know much about her personal life.

I never saw her again. Finally, I admitted to myself she was gone. But for years, when I allowed myself to think about her, I'd pretend she'd had some terrible accident that prevented her from contacting me. Admitting she'd changed her mind about our relationship was just not an option for me at the time."

I knew all about pretending, just hollow hope. "Did you know where she came from?"

"No. I was so happy with her, how she'd awaken a part of me I'd never experienced; I lived in the moment wringing every bit of juice out of our time together. When I think of her, I still envision all that thick hair." Eyes closed, his sadness was evident as he shared these memories. "I loved running my fingers through it."

"When did you let go?"

He hunched his shoulders and a stillness came over him as though he was trying to recall the moment, but he never answered the question.

"What about the other girl?"

"Memphis was her home. She was a different kind of girl, just the opposite of the one who stole my heart. My feelings for her didn't take root. She never made any demands on me, took things as they presented themselves, like the women in my family. I remember once when I wanted to change our plans, I called her and she said, 'No problem, I'll meet you, that way we'll have more time together.' How many women would respond with that ease?"

"Not many."

"It was never a relationship meant to last, though. Her neediness was not something I'd take on for very long. I moved on. But I do know, there is one woman out there somewhere who carries warm memories of me and when they cross her mind, they're sure to make her smile."

Now as I think back to that last visit, I feel an added sense of anger with myself. Our conversations about women always seemed to revolve only around my conflicting feelings concerning Kena, Rita and even my mom. How selfish I must have been, not giving more attention to all those questions he asked about them. That there had been a special woman in his past and he continued to carry intense feelings for her, was no idle admission. He wanted me to know, even at that late time in his life, we had a parallel experience in common, uncertainty about the important women in our lives. Why didn't I insist he tell me more about the special girl?

There were longer periods of silence during that final visit. He must have also been thinking about other inconsistencies in his life that could never be resolved, maybe even his choice to break all contact with his family. We spent more time than usual talking about Deon. He wanted more details. How was he doing in school? When would I see him again? Would he spend any time soon in New York with me?

"Why all these questions?" I asked him.

"With so many empty hours, sometimes, just to get through them, I establish a topic to think on. Lately, I've been thinking about fatherhood. Neither one of us had a father's influence in our lives, therefore, I can use my imagination."

"Whoa," I stopped him, "Your dad lived with you. He was there frequently. Our situations were very different."

"Would your life have been any different with your father in the house?"

Since this was a question I'd asked myself over the years, I responded without hesitation. "I would have known more about my mother and what made her tick."

"Don't confuse things, we're talking about your dad."

"I understand, but I know he could shed light on her motives and behavior."

"What else?"

"He would have established my place in the family: maybe relationships with cousins, aunts and uncles."

"How would that have changed things?"

"The opportunity to travel with him outside of Sero and visit with other people. I often wondered how it would feel to have a stake in a group of people who had responsibility for me as a child of the family."

"You had Grandma Neetha. Did she ever make you feel unwelcome?"

"No, but at the beginning she sure scared the hell out of me. For years it was just my mom I wanted. Only after I'd been in Sero for several years did I begin to wonder about my father. I never saw him until I'd been with Grandma for five or six years. I didn't know why he came. He was only with us for two or three days."

~

The undertaker I arranged to retrieve Billy's body provided as much dignity as anyone dying in a state prison can have. His last ride was in a late model hearse, not the usual battered panel truck owned by the state. I made no attempt to notify any family members. There was no evidence that any relatives ever visited him. I decided his last arrangements would be in Jackson as that was the only place he seemed to carry special memories. He was cremated. I paid extra for a local pastor to say final words during an abbreviated service at a funeral home attended by the pastor's wife, a few other church members and myself. They were strangers extending charity. The lawyer who represented him at trial also attended. Apparently, Billy maintained contact with him, still engaging those he chose.

The intimate service gave me a chance to say goodbye amid the turmoil and conflict of losing a person who was like blood to me. There were extra flowers I assumed I'd also paid for, but the funeral director informed me two of the arrangements had been left the night before. The undertaker said a woman had come by earlier and left these flowers. She didn't leave her name. That was not unheard of. People sometimes stop by funeral homes to pay their respects to the dead they've never met, especially in the south. There was no identification, just the short note 'Rest in Peace.'

After the short service, I drove to Sero and spread his ashes along the crumbling levee in the same area we so often set and discussed everything under the sun. *Who will help me figure out all the issues that haunt me now?*

I never had any type of relationship with Billy's family, so there was nothing to close the door on with them. When I left town, I drove by his house and saw nothing had changed. It stood decrepit and forlorn. The porch was still leaning to one side, but not as much as I remembered. They must have attempted repairs. His mother was absent from her permanent place on it.

Billy's death marked the end of my Sero life. There were no bonds left holding me there. I decided to sell the house and make an offer to the current tenants. They've taken good care of the property and if they want it, my offer will be a price they can afford. When I drove up to our house, I paused, not getting out of the car. I wanted to imprint the picture of my childhood home in my mind. It is likely the last time I see it.

Driving back to the airport, as always, I kept my eyes on the speed limit, reminded of Grandma's constant warning not to do anything that put myself in the spotlight of the law. That advice to me as a boy is not strong enough for me as a man. Just watching the speedometer was no protection. Out on these back roads it doesn't matter that I make decisions for thousands of people around the world. On these lonely asphalt strips, I am only a black man to be feared and destroyed.

The painful decision I'd made that Sero belonged only in my past was not the final word. I'd laid to rest the two most essential people from an important part of my life and thought I could take my memories and be done. But as it turned out, Sero was not ready to let me go.

The thick brown envelope from Billy's attorney arrived two months after his death. It contained a smaller sealed letter-sized envelope from Billy. After staring at the envelope far longer than reasonable, the feeling of finality saddened me, and I wanted to delay reading the letter inside. But there was no way to prevent this important door in my life closing.

The letter remained unopened until the next day, when with trepidation I slowly broke a corner of the envelope. Still reluctant to read what I feared to be more surprises, I finally tore it open across the top. It was dated three weeks before Billy died. A blend of loss and closure settled around me as I saw the familiar handwriting and remembered his sad face at the end of our last visit. His written words started as he always did, going straight to the point.

> I know everything is well with you, my man. You're always at the top of your game. As you can see from the note at the top, my lawyer, accepted this letter and promised to make sure you received it after my demise.
>
> We made a good team. Although I'm done, your path is wide open. Now that you've resolved the nuisance affecting your career, remember to stay alert at all times. During our last couple of visits, I sensed you were slacking in your understanding of racial issues. Don't mistake all the smiles thrown your way for acceptance, some are masks, hiding ancient grievances.
>
> Your smarts were always evident. Even in the old days, the way you held your opinion until others revealed themselves was impressive. It is the survival

> skill I most often use in this hellhole. It gives me a measure of control, which I'm sure you know is power.

Yes, I do. I read on, trying to understand the words that set out Billy's final thoughts.

> Thanks for never cutting me loose because I chose the journey that led me here. I never felt any criticism or judgment from you concerning my underground activities. Even so, I know you gave it plenty of mind time. In spite of your busy schedule your visits were frequent and positive.

You were my only friend Billy and I didn't want to lose that connection. Your friendship aided my survival. But you never understood your own historical advantages and because of my need for permanent attachments, I gave no attention to anything that might pull us apart. I should have been more alert.

My thoughts continually turned to that final visit and Billy's determined roundabout efforts to explain his life. He probably knew his time was near and that the visit may be our last, so he wanted to say everything he felt needed to be said. "I took a wrong turn because I thought I could outsmart the system; I did for awhile." He hunched his shoulders before continuing, but he began to cough uncontrollably. After gaining control he seemed to slump into himself. "Once a person like me becomes a target, things move fast and it becomes hard to hold together a disciplined team. My link with the crew became wider and weaker. It was just a matter of time before we were rounded up and arrested. And me, I landed in this government space."

I wasn't sure if that particular conversation was his attempt to put forth regrets in the artful manner he often expressed himself or if he'd really reached a point in which he was truly sorry for taking the low road. Another thing that puzzled me was a particular statement he made, "I will be grateful to you until the day I die, for taking ownership of our pact of brotherhood."

It was strange to hear that for I was always grateful to him for being the friend very few people have. From far away a fading voice argued, "He put your freedom in jeopardy. He brought his ill-fated activities right into the heart of the life we created. You were part of his scheme all along."

No.

He charted his own path always showing a disdain for convention, living his life without regard to family boundaries or customs. His comfort with risky behavior should have been something I noticed earlier. He was walking toward that prison door, one step at a time, probably his entire life. When we were kids his devil-may-care attitude was such a part of him, it didn't raise any alarms. In our part of the world, the roles we were assigned covered up aberrations that may have stood out prominently in other places. There was no room for anyone to care whether a white boy stayed away from home most of his waking hours, one who didn't adhere to his role in the family structure and most unusual, who chose a black boy as his best friend and constant companion.

I, on the other hand, was assigned the role of a black boy who must pay attention to rules, just to stay in Sero. One slip and out the door I'd go. I thought I knew all the rules, but at the time didn't understand the power of rules enforced by memory. The memory of another black boy in another town, not far away who paid the ultimate price, was firmly established in Grandma's memory. But for Billy, there was no need to rely on memory.

I don't know how long I set nursing those random thoughts, but I returned to that final visit and the efforts I made to hold back my recurring feelings of hurt and anger. More than forty years of living taught me to tamp down any show of emotion when the grasp of incoming information hinged on a single breath or the blink of an eye. But deep down in a place inside of me, confusion clawed, still seeking release.

The lawyer included his own brief hand-written note: Mr. Cady had a son. He lives with his mother at 324 Morningside Terrace on the west side of Jackson. It was his desire that you be informed.

A pounding noise in my ears began at the same time my heartbeat escalated dangerously. *Son? Billy has a son?* The words blurred. My mind unable to accept them. This had to be more of Billy's games.

For days I would not permit myself to touch the possibility. But it was like a wound that wouldn't heal, I had to consider the truth of this revelation; a child, his son. Why would he keep it secret?

All those times I sat talking about Deon his thoughts were on another little boy he'd never seen, but who carried his love. He was unable to know his son's daily routine: school, relations with his maternal family, his heroes and all the other parts of a young boy's life a father knows. With only his imagination to provide answers, Billy must have taken his clues from me and all my talk about my own son. Wow. And his mother, did she think about the man she'd once loved and allowed briefly into her life?

Once my mind finally accepted this startling information, I wondered if the boy had Billy's features or did he look more like his mother. Is he smart like his father? What questions did he ask his mother about his dad? Billy was more than six feet tall. Did this boy have the potential for Billy's height?

Immediately I calculated the child's age. Billy had been behind bars for ten years, so his son has to be somewhere between ten and eleven, about the same as Deon. This started me thinking again about Billy at that age. His leadership abilities were evident, even back then: grounded by the assumption that all his friends would follow him. And mostly we did.

Instantly I made a decision, as I'm sure Billy intended, to see this boy and his mother. Whether she cares to know about Billy's life after she left, does not matter. It is her son who has a right to know everything about his father.

16

When I arrived at the house and turned off the motor, I set in the car for a few minutes wondering about my reception. Like its neighbors the house was small and well kept. It was an old fashion craftsman style with a covered porch across the front. The pearl grey siding and dark blue shutters spoke of quiet elegance. This crisp look made it special. The yard was neatly trimmed with shrubbery that didn't overwhelm the inviting entrance. The house presented a confident face to the world. The scene enticed me.

I'd written to her, introduced myself and asked if she'd see me. She wrote back immediately agreeing to the visit. Curiosity grew as I mentally prepared myself for more surprises. What did she look like? After all these years I had no idea of Billy's type. Did he prefer tall women, those with curves or slim ones? What did she know about me? Experience had taught me most first-time meetings were awkward, therefore I also prepared myself for possible rejection. No matter the reception, my anticipation was intense.

I walked up the steps and rang the bell; the door swung open immediately. She must have seen me drive up. I was surprised. My assumption was not for an easy entrance.

"Brenda?" I reached out to shake her hand.

Her open smile welcomed me like an old friend.

"And you're surely T.J."

I couldn't help myself, I just stared. She was breathtaking. Her eyes so clear they were like mirrors. Prominent cheekbones highlighted her full lips that held promises of treats to come. A sly smile lit her face. I wasn't ready for my reaction to her. Whatever I expected to find here was overtaken by my immediate physical response.

In an instant my expectations changed. Standing before me was a woman I wanted to know in every way. The duties I owed Billy held firm, but my overwhelming instant attraction to this woman was my own.

It never occurred to me she would not be a white girl and Billy never let on. She appeared to be biracial, more black than white.

"Not exactly what you expected?" Her smile began to ease the concerns I had about meeting her.

"I never permit expectations to lay in wait, ready to jump out and sabotage a new relationship."

She stepped aside. "Come in."

Once inside, I quickly saw the interior was as tidy as the outside.

"I hope it meets your approval."

What response could I make? Clearly, she had some idea I'd come to judge her. I let the statement pass.

"Have a seat and I'll get you something cool to drink."

While she was out of the room, I had a more thorough look around. It reflected a taste that couldn't be defined as any one type of style. The furniture was neutral and comfortable. The pale walls made the room appear larger than its true size. If I were forced to put a name to it, I'd say it was leaning toward contemporary.

The sweet tea she gave me was slightly laced with mint. "We meet at last. I knew this day would come, but I didn't have any idea it would be after the person both of us cared for had passed."

Not a shy person. "Billy was full of surprises. After so many years of sharing our lives, it was only a couple of months before he died that he spoke of an important woman in his life and it turns out he was talking about you. I must admit, his revelation stunned me."

"My guess is he didn't really tell the whole story. I can see it in your face." Not once did her eyes shy away from mine.

"Your guess is right on. I haven't satisfied myself why he withheld such important information."

"You knew him longer than I and at a different level. The difference between the person you knew and the one I met was just the passage of time. The Billy I knew was a man unto himself, traveling this world as he pleased."

Don't push. "If you're comfortable, I'd like to hear more about that time in his life."

Without hesitation she began her story. "We met in a fast food place. I ordered and when I turned around to find a seat, I saw him and asked to join him. His smile was seductive and disarming. It was the only answer I needed. From that day forward I had no reservations about my time with him. He was as comfortable with me as I with him. We sparked. Billy was a fantastic conversationalist. There were no subjects he was reluctant to tackle."

"True, even during our earliest days, his intellect could have taken him anywhere he wanted to go."

"It did. Billy made the choices he wanted to make."

At that moment a shadow crossed her face, so brief and faint, I thought I might have imagined it. There was more to know about their time together. I wanted to hear everything she had to say. This beautiful woman sitting across from me had the final word on him. The secret of his time with her must have nourished him during the dark times and certainly in his final days. Maybe he did want to share it with me, but so many of our discussions settled on my life and concerns. Why did I assume there had not been a special corner of his life worth discussing with me? All the hours we spent together in that dreary building, he held close a secret too precious to chance having it trampled on or criticized?

"Shall I continue?"

"Please." Playing around the edges of my mind was continuing hope for information that would explain Billy's actions against me. Did she know something?

"We began seeing each other regularly. I looked forward to being with him as I'd never been with anyone else. It may surprise you that his race didn't matter."

"Oh no, he didn't live by conventional norms."

"Actually, his being white tantalized me, somehow it made him even more attractive. I was never afraid to be seen with him. We discussed this most important difference. He was bold and unconcerned."

"That was Billy, nothing fazed him."

"We were so close that sometimes now I can still remember his smell, his eyes that never closed when we made love."

The air in the room stilled. For the first time she lowered her eyes, I'm sure remembering a special time for her. After taking a deep breath she continued.

"This is the first time I've spoken of this special corner of my life. Usually when I return to those memories, it is to add a little joy to my day. I'm speaking frankly to you because I know what you meant to him. He talked about you like a person talks about his brother. It was often, 'T.J. and I did this, or T.J. says this, or T.J. can arrange that.' There came a time he told me that if I ever needed to, for any reason, I could call on you, at 212-236-7856."

"That still holds true." *Why did you never call?*

"And your grandmother was important to him. He said she was a force to be reckoned with. He even told me why you're called T.J."

"I shortened my name to T.J. my first day at school. It had an important sound. The teacher had asked each child his name. I wanted to feel important. Grandma Neetha called her boss Mr. W.B., never Mr. Boone, so it seemed to me an important person could be referred to by initials. From that day on I began to refer to myself as T.J. There were times when I was called by my first name and did not even answer because I thought the caller was referring to someone else."

Her voice was soothing and her smile seductive. While listening to every word, I waited to hear why Billy didn't trust me with this secret. We'd shared so many throughout our lives. *Why Billy? Why couldn't you tell me?* "As sure as we're sitting here, he intended us to meet one day and share our stories. Go on."

Old remembrances poured from her as if she'd been waiting for the right time to tell their story. "He was kind and thoughtful, always noticing little things; my nail polish or lipstick color. Even the coarse texture of my hair intrigued him. He never tired of stroking and running his fingers through it."

I remembered his voice softening when he spoke of a woman with thick curly hair. "Billy paid attention to details. How long were you together?"

"Almost a year."

"What happened?"

"Unintended consequences, roadblocks, life."

I waited, understanding she would speak at her own pace. When she began again, the pain was clearly visible as she rose from the chair, walked to the window and turned around. "T.J., I want you to know I loved Billy in a way that frightened me. I reached a point in our relationship where I wanted him to own me. I was just that taken with him. I don't know if you've ever loved that way, but it is dangerous.

He had a way about him I'd never seen in a man. When we were together, he made me his woman. He kept me close to him, sheltered me with his body so the world knew where I stood with him. He could have asked anything of me, and I would have complied. That was the danger."

She turned her back to me and looked out the window. I leaned forward, straining to hear her next words.

"When we made love, I ceased to live. I died second by second. The probable consequence of this recklessness caused me to run, to disappear, to be gone. While I was still able to, I took his love, his spirit and his son."

I could wait no longer. "How did he find out about his son?"

Before answering, she returned to the chair, sitting at the edge. "Let me go back a bit. First, I need to tell you this. His lawyer found me: tracked me down, really, and sent a letter. I went to see him, and he told me about Billy's situation."

"Did he say whether Billy asked to see you?"

"No. He hadn't asked. I'm sure he didn't want me to see him in his circumstances. And I'm not sure I would have agreed to see him even if he'd asked me to. I wanted only the good memories to carry with me and pass on to his child. I've often wondered if he intended for me to make the decision whether or not to visit him."

"Did the lawyer know about the child?

"Oh yes. He had all the information available about me. I was dumfounded when he told me the whole story of Billy's troubles, but I needed to know every detail of his life after our time together, no matter how sordid. His lawyer explained everything to me, leaving out nothing. That was Billy's advice to him."

"It was the lawyer who told you of his death?"

"Yes."

I had no reason to believe he ever saw his son, but I asked anyway, "Did he ever see the boy?"

"No, he never saw him."

"Brenda, why?"

"I couldn't stomach the possibility of having my child rejected for the same reason my father left my mother. My mother was a black woman who also fell in love with a man like Billy."

"A white man?"

"Yes. When she told him I was on the way, he left never to be seen again. It broke my mother's spirit. She never recovered. When I was twelve years old, she took her life. All

I could see in my future with Billy, was suffering, leading to a hopeless end. I had to walk away while I still held a tiny bit of myself capable of making decisions concerning a man who already owned me."

Conflicting statements flooded my mind. She'd meant more than most to him, but hearing her tell of their time together was unsettling. "How old is your son?"

"Eleven. If you can stay for a while longer, you'll meet him. He's at school."

"I cannot leave without meeting him. What's his name?"

"He's named after his father."

Hurt, anger and frustration descended on me at once. *How could Billy have this parallel life and I not know about it? He knew every detail of my life.*

"Does he ask about his father?"

"Frequently, now that he's older."

"And what do you tell him?"

"His father had some trouble and needed to leave the area. He's a child, for now he accepts this explanation."

"He doesn't know he's dead?"

"No."

Like a long struggling athlete, rising in strength, anger began to emerge from my other conflicting feelings. I wasn't sure if it was because Brenda had stolen from Billy or my own selfishness had robbed him of the opportunity to share his memories of the only golden days of his life. Then hurt began to replace anger followed by frustration.

"What will you tell him?"

"I don't know. My memories are of love between a man and woman. Those do not provide answers for a child who wants to know his father. If I knew what his family was like, I could share that information with him, but Billy never talked about his family. It didn't bother me because I needed all our time together to be about us. You and your Grandmother were the only people from his home he ever mentioned. He cherished both of you."

"It wasn't his way to share his immediate family life, not even with me. Unlike most people, he didn't seek sustenance from his family. They allowed him as much freedom as he determined fit his needs. But I'm sure he would have been a proud father. He was all the things you named, kind and thoughtful. Create memories for your son."

We discussed so many things that day about Billy I felt we were at last commemorating his life. I was able to fill in some of the blanks for her. The only other person who discussed him with me was Grandma and her words were always tinged with caution and suspicion. As we talked, Brenda expressed concern about her son's place in the world. "He's already bumped heads with his racial identity. Some of his classmates play ugly, taunting him. 'What are you, black or white?' How can I provide an answer? He has to choose if he wants. I wait and worry."

I was mesmerized by her deep feelings. She didn't hold back. As she spoke, I clearly felt her warmth and unbridled passion to love a man. Billy really did have a precious nugget of memories that were available to see him through all those tough days he endured.

Finally, the front door opened and a boy, tall for his age, came into the room. Speechless, I stared at him. I was, again, looking into the pale gray eyes I remembered. The way he held his head, slightly to the right as if quizzing someone and the smile that spread so easily across his face,

I had seen so many times. Even the hair color was the same, thicker than Billy's, but the mixture of brown with strands of deep blond were identical. He could pass if he chose that route. Billy's boy. *He would have enjoyed every minute with you.*

"This is T.J."

"Hi." His voice held a question and his eyes never left mine, but he extended his hand, giving me a firm grip.

"Have your snack. T. J. will be here for awhile."

As I watched him leave the room, I knew this visit would not be my last. I must get to know this child and be to him whatever he needs. The initial shock of his existence still had not settled.

"Will you tell him who you are?"

"Absolutely, if it is okay with you."

When Bill returned, I saw more of his father, how his eyes looked directly into mine, still with a question.

His mother didn't avoid opening the subject of his father. "T.J. knew your dad. They were friends, even when they were boys."

He came and sat next to me. "What did he say about me?"

Like his mother I wasn't prepared to answer that question at the moment. "I was five years old when I first met him. He was also five. Our friendship was immediate. Billy, that's what I called him, was outgoing, not a shy person. He could talk about anything."

He interrupted me "When did he say he would come to see me and Mommie?"

"He didn't say, but I need to tell you more." I felt constricted because he had a right to know his father was gone forever, but he also needed to have a clear sense of Billy the man, before he could absorb the knowledge of his death. I, too, had to get beyond many of the revelations I learned since entering their home.

The boy's eyes never left mine. "I want to see him."

"Let T. J. finish."

I knew I could, honestly, assure him of his father's love, so I didn't hold back. "He can't come to you now, but he always had you and your mother on his mind. He wanted you to do well in school. How're you doing?"

"My grades are good."

"Very good," Brenda emphasized.

"Your dad was smart too, he made top grades all through school."

I was running out of generalities to say about his father. Putting off the truth was not getting easier. He would never see his father. He deserved the truth. I put my arm around his shoulders and said as gently as possible, "Your dad is gone son. He passed away more than two months ago." I looked for any signs that he felt hurt, anger or maybe betrayal, but surprisingly, he was ahead of us.

"I wondered about that since I never saw him. Someone in my class had a father who died, and our teacher explained it to us."

"Do you understand you will never see him now?"

"Yes, but I want you to tell me more about him."

"And I will. What do you want to know?" I breathed a sigh of relief. Brenda and I were off the hook for now.

The first question concerned a physical description of his father. "What did he look like?"

"Very much like you. Your gray eyes are identical to his. So is the dark golden color of your hair." I waited for him to continue, thinking the questions would indicate what was on his mind.

"Did he cut his hair the same?"

"Almost."

"Everyone says I'm tall, was he tall?"

"Yes, very tall."

"We are twins then."

"You and your dad are very much alike."

During this exchange Brenda sat without moving. From the corner of my eye I saw her clasped hands in her lap and wondered what she must be thinking at this moment. My answers seemed to satisfy the boy for now and he left the room.

"This means so much to me, to have him get to know his father from someone who knew him before we met: to have a man's perspective."

"It's a real pleasure to bring his dad to life for him. When I think about things, Billy must have known, at some time in the future it would be my job to pass on the crux of his life: good and bad."

"Please. Hold back nothing and neither will I."

I couldn't help wondering how Billy managed a relationship with such a self-assured woman while also running an intense illegal drug operation.

"The very first conversation we had was about health and food. I remember his words exactly, "You'll ruin your good looks eating so much fried food."

She was going deep and the memories briefly stopped her narrative. Before she could breathe another breath, I asked to take them to dinner.

"Thanks for caring," Her response was accompanied by a smile that covered me with a sweet warmth. I felt I'd won an unexpected prize. It's that same feeling a man gets when out of the blue a woman comes on to him and they both enter the game for whatever it brings. Our connection caught fire at that minute. I was all in.

"Billy was the kind of person who jumped over niceties and filters, aiming straight for the bull's eye."

Bill went outside to play with friends. He had no homework for the weekend. Brenda and I talked on, as time slipped by quickly. Neither of us wanted to end this first meeting. It was getting late and I needed to catch a plane, but she suggested I spend the night with them. I accepted.

At five o' clock Bill came in and we left for the restaurant. As I'd agreed to stay with them overnight, we didn't rush. I welcomed the day's end, needing time to digest so many of the new factors I'd learned about my old friend. As it turns out he had for, at least a short time, a period of normalcy.

The day of surprises wound down and finally each of us headed to bed filled with new insights about Billy. I lay in bed trying to process all the new information. It would not be easy. I now had a reason to legitimately hang onto the past with Billy: the new connection with Brenda and their son. In my last conversation with him there were signs of secrets. He was less free flowing, more focused on my relationship with Deon. I thought he seemed to be comparing it to the almost nonexistent relationship he had with his father. Now I understand it wasn't only his father, it was also his son. "How often does Kena say Deon asks about you?" His question seemed so out of place at the time, but nothing was ever off the table between us.

"She doesn't. He has permission to call whenever he pleases. There are no restrictions on his contact with me.

I refuse to have him learn to accept me only on my terms, as I had to do with my father who I only saw twice. I would have him come to me more often, if I didn't travel so much."

"I can understand that. I'd want a different relationship than the one I had with my own father." He was quiet for a moment before continuing, "And I saw him two or three times a week. I know your child support payments are more than generous."

"It's financial maintenance, not child support. He and his mother are my family and they will have every material desire they can imagine. I'll never see them live with the demands of an inadequate budget."

"You know, even in here some of these guys keep their relationships with their children going. Some of them actually have visits. I once thought it was foolish. This is a place for long term. I didn't see any purpose in having visits with children, but I guess it does give a father hope that his child will not go down the same road."

Even though he didn't give me the true story, he set in motion the process that would lead me to his son. His lawyer's directions assured it. His expectations were that I'd do whatever is required to assist his son. *And I will.*

Staring at the ceiling; thinking of Billy with Brenda, I tried to see her as she appeared in his eyes. I could not. My body only permitted me to see her dark eyes, soft skin and inviting smile. I couldn't overcome my body's reaction to the thought she was in bed in the room next door, just steps away.

Saturday morning as we shared breakfast, Brenda announced she had errands to take care of and we'd be on our own for a few hours. "How would you like to spend a couple or three hours with T.J.?"

He answered quickly, "I want you to see my school."

"We'll do whatever you like." I was gratified she trusted me with her son, allowing me time to reveal as much of his father's life as I felt appropriate. We started our adventures two hours after his mother left and, of course, our first stop was the school. We walked around the building and ended on the playground. He loved geography, decimals and basketball. Not far from the house we stopped at the recreation center where he was a member of the swim team.

"I see you really love sports. You play any other games?"

"Sometimes baseball when we can get enough players. What sports did my dad play?"

"He was not so much into sports. In our small town there were no organized sporting activities." In case he was disappointed, I added, "Like you, he probably would have played basketball."

We wandered around the neighborhood and then went to the library where he and I played computer games. He was good at them, very quick. By the time we returned home, his mother was preparing a snack. Three hours later I was driving back to the airport. The visit had lifted my spirits and provided another unexpected link in my chain of luck or chance: too early to tell which it is.

17

A year ago, the smooth flow of my life was shattered. I was consumed by Greg's eventual arrest, Billy's treacherous actions and subsequent death. Even though the problem with Greg is resolved, I remain super vigilant that as a consequence of someone else's behavior, my career can be destroyed in an instant. Then I think about Grandma's flight from her childhood home, running for her life and still able to move on from that peril. "Survival has many levels. It means more than getting from one day to the next. The footsteps of your journey must be clear enough so they can be seen by the person behind you." She was surely thinking of Deon. I must do the same and put away these unreasonable fears. Then there is also this new existence without Billy's place in it. I'm moving forward, with no roadmap showing me how to proceed with the two people he left behind who are now part of my life.

After the initial visit, my need to see Brenda and Bill again brought me back to Jackson within weeks. They welcomed me as family and insisted I stay in their home. It seemed to be what they expected. I'd encouraged Bill to call me if he wanted additional answers about his father. He made two calls, asking about his dad's family. I explained they were still living in Sero. But I was not comfortable explaining Billy's complex relationship with them. He said he wanted to see them.

The structured life Brenda has created for her son is so different from his father's young life. Bill knows his mother's love, the meaning of every inflection in her voice and the many ways he makes her smile. No ambiguity. She is one of those rare women who knows what life requires of her and is comfortable with the decisions she makes. She brought Billy into her life and left him for reasons she found necessary and then went on to become a psychologist.

Reluctantly, I've begun to make comparisons between her, Kena and Rita. I'm intrigued by their differences. Kena tells me what she thinks pleases me. Rita often seems uncertain of her place in my life, so I don't really know her deepest feelings about the long-term possibilities of our relationship. Each one of them is okay settling for parts of me. My mother sometimes becomes a factor in these comparisons: her motives always mysterious. Brenda, on the other hand, is not a woman who settles, even in the face of hurt. She is always clear about her view of important situations in her life. I don't need to waste time figuring out her meanings. It is appealing. She does share one trait with Grandma, though, she doesn't forget lessons learned. Her early life is the textbook by which she lives today. She was well into that book when she met Billy. It's possible she could have assumed a different racial identity if she'd wanted, but for a little too much shading. Whether she ever wanted to or even tried, I don't know. She was intimately aware, however, of her mother's heartache. That may have frightened off any expectation of something different on the other side of the color line. When she met Billy, she was firmly on the side of living life as a black woman.

Squeezed in among our discussions of Billy, we talked about our families. Not knowing enough about my own mother's story nor Billy's mom's history, there was no information I could give Bill on what to expect from Ms. Cady. But because he may know enough of Brenda's early life, she didn't oppose a meeting with his father's people. When I suggested he meet them, she immediately agreed. She understood the value in knowing family history. Her son needed to be made whole and that could only happen if he learned as much about his father as he could from those who knew him best. Eventually the upcoming visit took on an urgency because of Bill's growing curiosity about the family.

My conversations with Brenda often led back to her time with Billy. I continued to struggle with her description of that part of his life. "After you made the decision to leave the relationship, did you ever have any regrets?"

She held herself close before answering, but when she did, the response was explosive, "Immediately."

"Why?"

"I missed his unconventional ways: the quick smile, the look of possession that brightened his face, most of all, the intensity of our time together. There was an ownership each of us had of the other, that was potent. It was the experience together I wanted; just to have the same sun shine on both of us. We reached a place where we didn't always need speech to affirm our bond: a touch or smile was sufficient."

Instantly a powerful feeling of jealousy swept through me. It frightened me because below the surface of the man

I knew was another man I didn't know and regret I couldn't see, that hidden Billy. "It is true, different rivers ran through him at different times in his life. But what you experienced with him I'm sure was part of the authentic Billy Cady." Grandma's voice intruded, just to keep the record clear, 'So how can you explain his not rescuing you earlier from that awful beating, and then sic'ing Greg on you? Was that the authentic Billy?' This time I had no answer.

"The only reason that makes any sense for keeping your relationship secret is he wanted it to be untainted by what anyone should think or say."

"I must accept what you say is the truth, that way I don't need to doubt the past."

"There are times when we set in stone remembered words spoken by people long gone that may be called into question by life itself. But we hold these words and even their actions sacred. The right thing to do now is to let the memories be as they are, not look behind them because of a present challenge." *I'm moving on Grandma.* "If you question a past decision, you may open the door to questions about your son. Be careful."

"These are complicated times, also incredibly good times for Bill and I since you came into our lives."

I was not, however, so readily prepared to admit their affect on me. I honestly couldn't put a name to my feelings, but with her I felt refreshed, new. Her eyes, words and smile spoke with one voice. Her eagerness to know more about Billy's life before she met him, never diminished. "Before our teen years we began making up situations and then providing solutions. He returned to that game during the last visits I had with him. He asked me, what would I think if he took up with a girl like Kena?"

"One who looked like her or one with her smarts?" I asked him. "It was important to flesh out as many facts as each could provide."

"Both," he responded immediately.

"You'd be a very lucky man. She has no faults."

"Faultless women don't exist. If you look hard enough, her faults will naturally reveal themselves. Sometimes just being a woman is the fault." *Was he thinking of you?*

"You're not making sense."

"If she's so perfect, why haven't you married her?"

"I never said she was perfect. She is a woman who would lift any man's life."

"I ask you again, why isn't she your wife?"

"He was pushing the game and determined to get an answer even though we'd discussed the subject many times."

"He played that game with me too. 'What if we were committed in marriage?' he asked me.

"How would marriage change things? I threw back to him. He didn't answer. I'd already begun to feel our relationship could go no further. It was shortly after that particular conversation I made the decision to walk away. It was heart-rending. Basic instinct kicked in. I knew a marriage commitment with its oppression waited just around the corner."

"How were you able to stand against all his efforts to locate you?"

"Of course I knew of his full-court press to find me. But I couldn't give in. I was not emotionally able to allow a false step to enter the relationship."

"Why is the possibility of marriage a false step?"

"It interrupts the flow of the journey. My feelings for Billy were total, but to allow a marriage commitment to lay down a new set of arrangements was not something I would do."

"How do you know he wasn't just exploring possibilities?"

"I don't know. I was not willing to lose what we had for a gamble on chance."

Is that why I will not commit more to Kena? "You knew him as a man of his word. Where was your trust?"

"We trusted the relationship to guide us. It was rock solid, but marriage has a way of boxing the parties in, placing the weight of outside circumstances heavily on their backs. Carrying that weight then becomes the only reason for holding the marriage together. The initial reason for the attraction takes a back seat. The purpose and passion present at the beginning of the relationship disappear. Then hurt and self protection become the rulers." Gathering old thoughts and hurts, she continued, "I'd seen what happens to a woman when she gives herself totally to a man. My experience taught me he will trample that self she gives him. I made a painful decision. Memories of joy are easier to carry than reminders of pain that live forever."

"But pain has its own place. Its memory takes us back to the beginning, to the lesson that must be remembered." *Often again and again.*

Our talks grew more intimate as we peeled away the layers that Billy laid down to mask much of his truth. She was not surprised he'd put his superior intellect to work in fashioning a long-range plan for success in an illegal trade. He was not afraid of risk, but didn't understand their relationship, itself was a risk. Their bond, however, held fast in her memories. No danger it would change, now that I am in the mix.

I wanted to know more details. "What has your life been like all these years?"

"When I met Billy, I was navigating all the requirements of college. I finished school and started my career. I hope one day to have my own practice when the time is right. Seeing after Bill is my most important task now. Fortunately, I landed a job immediately after graduation. My cousin helped me look after him until I could arrange childcare."

I noticed she never mentioned her finances, but it's clear she's holding her own financially: a woman of property. Unexpectedly, I wondered if there was a man in the background helping out. *Why am I looking for weakness in her?*

Her eyes held mine as our give-and-take continued. We were conspirators revealing bits of knowledge known by one and not the other. Billy, the brother to me was also the man who harbored secrets so deep I had trouble absorbing all of them. "Where were you hiding during all the time he looked for you?"

"I left Jackson and went to Chicago to stay with my cousin's close friend. I stayed until she thought it was safe to return. I knew he would not give up easily. That's where Bill was born."

"No, he did not. But he was a realist and I'm sure he finally convinced himself your relationship would go no further."

Putting the pieces together, I had confirmation he really did continue his operations, including business in Memphis. Staying in the background, he was able to hold himself apart from the group leaving them to believe he was a low-level functionary, not the brains behind the organization.

18

I was spending less time with Rita: my mind being consumed with sorting through all the new information I'd learned about Billy from Brenda. I needed time to fit the pieces of this puzzle together. Seeing him through her eyes made him more human, more vulnerable. The man I thought had an answer for everything had real trouble sorting his own life. Would a life with Brenda have rescued him from his illegal journey? A woman can have a powerful influence on a man, transforming him beyond what he himself thinks he's capable of becoming. During that last visit he asked more specific questions about the amount of time I spent with Deon. Was he at last questioning the road he'd chosen?

Even with the onslaught of more inconsistences about Billy, I could not ignore my growing desire to spend more time with Brenda. But my creeping male interest in her also fueled a new and unexpected ambivalence about staying with Rita. The simmering excitement she created produced a pleasant edge to our interactions. I embraced it.

She continued to up my expectations, always direct and never backing away from the many topics we discussed, even ones we stumbled into. She was concerned about Bill's desire to visit his grandmother and her reaction to him. "What if Ms. Cady rejects him?"

"He has to learn rejection is someone else's opinion of the situation. It changes nothing for him. That was Billy's way of thinking."

"Maybe not. Billy wasn't always immune to what others were thinking about him."

Another domino falling. "You continue surprising me."

"It's his woman speaking, but his brother listening, different translations."

She was quiet for a moment as if deciding whether to launch her next shot. She finally spoke, with a hidden smile hovering deep in her eyes. "How you would think about our relationship was always on his mind. Not that it would change anything, but it was important you should support us."

Before any expression of surprise showed on my face, she quickly continued. "Your relationship with Rita didn't bother him, he just wasn't sure you were prepared to accept me. It really worried him."

"While I was constantly seeking his support for my decisions, he did not trust me enough to count on my support for the few decisions he was still able to make." I felt disappointment and anger. I can only make it up to him by doing what he couldn't do for his son. The stillness in the room held its breath, waiting to hear more. Taking her hand gently I promised, "To stand for him."

"I know you will."

The growing closeness was sweet, each step to be savored. I had to be honest with myself. Was I doing only what Billy would want? I felt an urgency to make them a part of my life, so we began preparing his son to meet the other side of his family in four weeks. I decided to make no announcement of our coming, we'd just show up and let matters unfold naturally. The prospect of meeting these new people excited Bill as he began to ask questions. "Are there any children my age living in the house? Is their house like mine? Did my dad tell them about me?"

Since I was the only one who had answers, his questions were always directed to me. But his mother listened carefully, she too wanted answers and I needed to allay her fears about the upcoming visit with his grandmother, "He's three-fourths white, what can she say?"

"She doesn't need to say anything. Unsaid words can have life-long tentacles, especially when a child expects to hear he's loved and accepted. These people weren't the greatest parents to his father, so there is no reason for them to accept the child of their son. You know that. I grew up being sensitive and alert to other people's words and potent silences. They can bury themselves in a child's psyche."

"Even though Billy was always on his own, what influences he did or didn't receive at home affected his cavalier behavior toward life. When you tapped into a part of him that was so vulnerable, he had no reference for protecting himself, so he just kept opening his heart to every moment. And it overwhelmed you." *Must I explain Billy's behavior forever?*

Before meeting Brenda and Bill, I concluded there was no reason for me to return to Sero. I carry with me Grandma's resilient hopes and even Billy's tilted persistence in moving toward a goalpost he couldn't see. Keeping those memories, as I lived them, locked safely away in my heart is comforting. I can draw on them any time I need to affirm my own life.

I had two additional visits with them before taking Bill to meet his grandmother. For the first time I'd see Sero through the eyes of someone who has never been there. The part of my life I thought over was, instead, expanding. Sero was not ready to let me go. What aspect of his father's childhood was necessary for Bill to see? A brief shadow crossed Brenda's face as we prepared to leave. Pulling her close I held her longer than necessary. The feel of her softness and feminine scent almost overpowered me. With great effort I leaned back and looked for a sign of doubt in her eyes. Instead I saw surprise and anticipation.

~

The 150-mile trip took less than three hours. When we pulled up to the house Bill jumped out of the car the second I turned off the motor. There was no one in the yard and Ms. Cady was not on the porch. Bill ran up the steps while at the same time calling out, "Hello, anybody here?" Receiving no answer, he came back down to the yard. Then from the back of the house a group of children came running up to him. I was standing next to the car watching them.

"Hi," Bill spoke.

They continued staring at each other. No one from the group said anything. "Where's my Grandma?"

Grandma is a person known to all children, finally someone responded, "In the house."

Bill again ran up the steps and through the front door. "Grandma, I'm here."

Watching, I saw him establishing his dominance: no hesitation or uncertainty. Bill's entrance into this family was on his terms. Once he determined his grandmother was inside, he felt no need to wait for an invitation into her presence. Like his father, his sense of ownership was natural. *No matter what they think, he has rights to this place that, incredibly, is still standing.*

Ms. Cady led him back out onto the porch. "T.J., is this your son?"

"No." I hesitated for a second. "This is Billy's child, your grandson."

She came around in front of him and looked down at his face. Smiling, Bill looked up at her. She turned to me again. This time with a frown, not understanding. The other children had gathered at the foot of the porch also trying to unravel this riddle.

"I'm Bill," he told her.

"He's named after his father."

"Billy's boy?" She asked, still frowning down at him.

"That's right and he's come to meet you."

She slowly ran her fingers through his hair, then tipped his head back and began checking his face, rubbing a finger along his jaw, around his lips and leaned down to stare into his eyes. "Your eyes are gray too. Where do you live?"

"Jackson."

"And your mamma?"

It's time to establish the links. "He lives with his mom. They just learned about you. I convinced her Billy would want his son to know you and the other members of the family. It may be a hard pill for you to swallow at this moment, Ms. Cady, but he is your blood."

When she looked back at me, resignation had settled on her. She went to her chair and set down. I was sure the security of that chair would help in confronting the many thoughts that must be going through her mind. *Keep moving.* "Bill, you have anything to say to your grandmother?"

He'd already jumped from the porch and was back with the group of children watching him. "Who're you?" he asked the tallest.

"That's Waylon, your cousin," Ms. Cady announced from the porch. "And the others are his sisters and brothers. They're my grandchildren too."

"What were you doing around back?" Bill asked.

"Come and see," Waylon invited, and they disappeared around the corner of the house.

I took a seat at the foot of the porch and began the story Ms. Cady was waiting to hear. "Billy had a life beyond Sero. As close as we were, I only recently learned about Bill and his mother. Billy never told me about them. I can only guess at some point he would have."

"I'm not surprised. He never cottoned to anything or anyone here. For years we never knew where he was or what he was doing. After he was locked up, we were told, but he hadn't put us on the visitor's sheet, so we just kind of lost contact. I know he was ashamed of us." She hunched her shoulders and looked down at her clenched hands.

Because I didn't contact them when he died, I assumed she didn't know of his passing. But she did. The prison pipeline is tight and what happens behind bars has a way of seeping outside the walls. I needed to say something. She was his mother, a mother who, at least, saw him daily before he left home. They resided under the same roof. She had to mean something to him. He knew the trail I would follow was destined to lead back to this sorry plot of land.

"Ms. Cady, when Bill learned he had a grandmother, we could not contain his excitement. He needs to know you and the rest of the family. Look at him, how much he looks and even behaves like Billy."

"He looks like he could be Billy's child, every little thing I can see in him. What kind of woman is his mother?"

"A woman who also wants him to know the other side of his family. Billy loved her. He wanted to make their relationship permanent"

"How do you know all this when you said you just found out about them?"

Be careful. Stick to facts as they are. "She told me their story and you see he's the spitting image of Billy. And the last two times I saw him he made statements, as I look back, that should have been a signal he was holding a secret. Why he didn't talk about them to me, I can only think the whole idea of having a family was something too precious, too personal to share."

"Even with you?"

"Even with me."

"The two of you were thick as thieves, nothing we could do about it. Around here everybody was in the same situation. But you found a way to go. Billy couldn't."

"He did leave Ms. Cady."

"Straight to prison."

"No. He made it all the way to Memphis."

"You really don't know as much as you think."

So it seems.

"His cousin came up here and asked him to come down to Jackson, said he could find something to do. He was gone in a heartbeat."

"He never sought my help to find a way out."

"You never offered."

I assumed he would make his way as he wanted.

"I watched you two. He always looked up to you, even when you were little boys. We constantly heard his comparisons between your life and his. There was no way we could say he was wrong. Even though Ms. Neetha had high-handed ways, she had control of things, a nicer home of her own. Compare that to the chaos around here. Billy reminded us every chance he got that we were not as good as you and Ms. Neetha. Once he threatened to move in with you and her. Too many people in this house he would often say."

"I'm sure he was just kidding. He liked to get a rise out of people."

"T.J., listen to me." She stopped the rocking chair, before continuing, "Billy wanted your life, self confidence and ultimately the future you and Ms. Neetha made. We couldn't give him those things and he knew it. So, he resented living here."

It seems his mother knew more about his inner life than anyone suspected "He never spoke any words against his family."

"You knew him as a playmate and good friend. I knew him as a mother knows her child. Of course I knew he was smart. Billy started walking at nine months and was talking so we could understand him before his first birthday. Early on he had an independent spirit, most of the time playing alone, that is, until you came to Sero. He saw in you the person inside of himself. The person we could not reach."

Once again someone is talking about my best friend, my brother, but she is really telling me about myself. Was Billy just someone I took from to even out my own lonely life? Was this friendship so one-sided I was blind to its true dynamics? Was our brotherhood only a myth I constructed?

Ms. Cady kept talking while my thoughts slipped away: piercing questions coming forth demanding answers. As youngsters there was so much we didn't know that limited our imaginations. My plan lay in Grandma's imagination, but Billy was struggling to see adult life in Sero with zero guidance from his family. Then I heard her say, "His father was not pleased at the way he followed you around."

"What are you saying?"

"Every morning he'd announce his intentions to find out what your plans were for the day. It was like he was telling us we had nothing to offer him."

It's true the boundaries in his life were always fluid, defined by him alone. Being the arbiter of the choices and decisions he made, gave him an unusually high level of comfort for his style of independence. This confident attitude was one of the main attributes that fascinated me.

I heard the children's loud voices and immediately rose and headed toward the back of the house. "Let me check on them, to make sure they're not up to any mischief."

"No one ever checked on you all when you were growing up," she flung at me.

How wrong you are. Grandma's eagle eyes were always watching. While I was trying to blend in as a typical Sero boy, she knew it would never happen. She remained alert for the mixed messages of our relationship to explode. Did she see the vulnerable Billy? Is that why she rarely intervened?

Looking back, I should have seen his struggles. Being at home only when necessary; his house was just a place where he slept and sometimes ate. Often he followed me home to eat with us. Grandma always had enough food to share. He ate generously and always thanked her profusely. In the evenings he was slow to return to his house.

Our visit lasted into the afternoon. Bill's exuberance infected the other children. By the time we left a bond between them was in the making. Bill promised he'd come back and they could go exploring together.

"Uncle T.J. when can we come back?"

"We'll have another visit before school starts." I wanted to hear his impressions of the family, but I decided not to ask questions. I thought it better for him to reveal the visit and what it meant to him in his own way.

He was quiet as we drove away, then suddenly, he asked, "Do you have a boy?"

"Yes, he's near your age, eleven." I was glad he couldn't see my face. I was surprised by the question. I'd told Brenda about Deon, but never discussed him with Bill. Since meeting him, I'd given no thought to any similarities between them. He soon fell asleep and didn't awake until we were near home. Of course, he and Deon need to meet. They have a history unknown to them, with tentacles spreading beyond their everyday lives, connecting without direction by anyone, just by chance. No, it was luck going back years before their times. I will make the introduction happen, only after Bill's return trip to his grandmother's home. Ms. Cady and the other members of the family need to be firmly imbedded in his psyche prior to bringing another stranger into his life. I felt I was creating something new: maybe expanding my family. A bridge was now connecting the root of my life to a new path leading away from the accumulating mental clutter.

I felt a sense of pride. Bill's skill in taking control of the visit reminded me of one of my earliest days with his dad and how Billy exhibited similar dominating behavior. Several days after we met, he came down the road and walked past me. Intrigued, I followed him. We ended up under the tall tree at the corner. When we sat on the ground, he set with his back to the tree trunk and I was left to sit with little of its shade covering me. It didn't take many days for me to understand he was taking the power seat. The meaning of the term I was to learn later, but at that early age I understood that seat was the coveted one representing a higher status. From that day the power flowed back and forth between us. The first one to get to the tree took the seat.

Prioritizing the importance of integrating Bill into my life was the same as handling professional responsibilities: identifying the most important step, then taking action. Mentally it was comparable to being back in the office tackling, in turn, each matter in order of its importance. My first step is to let Kena know I'm bringing him out to California to meet Deon.

Brenda's relief, when we returned with good news that the visit had gone well, assured me we'd made the right decision. "You would have been proud of him. He stepped into a place that seemed to be waiting for him and filled the empty space Ms. Cady was holding open so many years for Billy to occupy.

Her failure to make a final farewell fits the person I remember, aloof and uncaring. But she was kind, even if curious, to Bill. The tone of his brief interactions with them was Billy come to life. He wasn't looking for acceptance. He was looking them over, satisfying his own curiosity. And Ms. Cady knew it. Her reality where Billy was concerned leaped to his son. It was a sight to behold. Even the cousins assumed a deferential attitude toward him, allowing him to lead their play.

Possibly he was finally helping her to realize a dream she had for her son which may now come true through her grandson. When he asked to see Billy's bedroom. Ms. Cady showed him the small room that had belonged to Billy and told him he could sleep there if he wanted. It was neat with a twin bed and dresser. Watching them together, I tried to recall observing a give-and-take conversation between Billy and his mom, but none came to mind. He rejected them for reasons of his own. With such a dominant personality, they left him alone, which permitted him to come and go as he pleased."

"Sometimes a mother and child communicate without words: an understanding voice or smiling eyes will do."

My surprise at hearing Ms. Cady's reflections on Billy's behavior caused me to wonder if she knew more about me than I ever considered. Is there some secret knowledge mothers have? I'd never really talked to Ms. Cady, but she had surprisingly expressed a mother's understanding of her son. While sitting on her front porch most of the day, apparently, she too was watching and evaluating our actions, resolving to wait and see. Another woman living with resolve. Is that how women live their lives? Grandma resolved to try one more time to make a man. Kena resolves to take whatever I give to her. Rita resolves to expect no more than what the day brings. What resolve did my mother make? And Brenda, what is the resolve I see in her eyes?

I wasn't ready to let Ms. Cady off the hook, just as I wasn't prepared to let my own mother off. All the years of comparing my mother's relationship with me to Grandma's, then Kena's way of interacting with Deon and now Brenda with Bill, did not allow me to see Ms. Cady in a more charitable light.

Secretly, I'd hope the trip back to Sero would lessen the sting of Billy's treachery, but it had not. My uneven emotions were heightened by the secret life he'd kept from me. Brenda saw in him something beyond what a woman sees in the man she loves. She'd discovered a more authentic Billy: the hidden person I didn't know existed. I felt jealous. With no outlet for these emotions, nagging questions continued. Was he really my brother? Was I a mere pawn in his game? Is this what Grandma observed?

As those emotions tormented me, so did my sneaking attraction to her. She turned to me, unconscious of this new dynamic. Today her looks were more potent then usual, but her words still hurt. "You had women in your life. Why did it never cross your mind, before he mentioned a special time, that somewhere in Billy's background, there could be a special woman?"

My voice hardened, challenging her. "We always talked about any subject as we wanted. It wasn't our practice to try and look for secrets. Whatever Billy wanted me to know, he would tell me: even the reasons for his apparent disdain for his family. I never questioned him about it."

She boldly threw back, "But brothers go beyond the obvious. Each knows when the other is holding a secret; indirect eye contact, a sideways glance, nervous hand movements or some other particular behavior observed over time."

I heard echoes of Grandma trying to get me to see the whole Billy, not only the parts I chose to acknowledge. My frustration would not allow me to accept the idea our entire friendship was one-sided. I was looking for answers that continued to elude me and her comments did not help. They made me question her objectivity. Was she holding other hurtful secrets?

19

Being back in the office was no protection against my growing attraction to a woman who excited every inch of me, despite her challenges to the validity of my bond with Billy. Imagining what it would be like to have her, kept interfering with my concentration. I tried, instead, focusing on nursing my anger against Billy's hurtful actions. It didn't work. Pictures of her beautiful face and thick black hair continued distracting my concentration on the important matters confronting me since my return. Frustration gripped me most of the day. But I moved through the hours with an outward calmness that belied my inner turmoil.

The following weekend I returned to Jackson. Warm feelings accompanied me as I eagerly looked forward to spending more time with her even knowing we'd have further painful discussions about Billy. When I arrived back at the home and walked into the house it felt familiar and intimate. She looked so soft and vulnerable. Unable to check my fascination with her, I felt it was time to, just let my emotions flow, holding back nothing.

Since I'd arrived near the end of the school day, I had more time to spend with Bill before he left for a weekend science camp. He was excited to see me, and I easily fell into, what was becoming a familiar role, answering his many questions about his dad, mostly, as a child his age. "Did he have after-school chores? What kind of games did he play? What were his favorite foods?" I had no trouble recalling those days, and Brenda allowed us the space for this precious time together. We were establishing a relationship I could not name, so I felt it necessary to let him know I'd be gone when he returned on Sunday.

After he left, an awkward silence settled between Brenda and me. I decided to use a group dynamics technique when discussion comes to a halt: throw a bomb into the group. "I'm itching to run my fingers through your hair."

Her beautiful eyes widen, and her lips parted. She crossed the room and set next to me on the sofa, an oversized loveseat, really. We were inches apart: so close I smelled her enticing scent. This new electric tension between us vibrated. Tilting her head back, I placed a hand on each side of her face, moving my fingers slowly through the springy strands. Looking deep into her eyes, I wanted an answer to my unspoken question. She responded by moving closer and cradling my face in her hands before briefly touching her lips to mine.

Several times today I'd caught her looking at me with a distinct hunger, before turning away. My own desire was building, unchecked, with slow intensity. I took her hand bringing it to my lips: holding it there, then placing a soft kiss on the inside of her palm. The slow simmering fire began to burn hotter as I felt the vibrations in her fingers. With great effort I checked myself, knowing I must not rush her.

Standing, I pulled her from the sofa, watching her reaction. "Come with me?' It was more than a question. I was barely holding onto my emotions when I turned and with my arms around her waist led her to my bedroom. Watching her, I wanted to savor every second as she slowly slid her top over her beautiful hair. Then her remaining clothes followed. I had imagined so many times the feel of her smooth, firm body. When I reached out and touched her, she gasped, and my tightly held control began to evaporate. Never taking my eyes from hers I pinched a nipple and watched her pupils widened so quickly, I thought she was surprised. I wanted to see her reaction again, so I gently pinched both nipples and watched the reaction again. I continued to check my own response, but my need took the lead. She would not be denied and greedily opened her mouth to mine, demanding more. Words and memories vanished. Then emotions that had no words took their places.

Moving slowly down the softness of her body into the void where only the two of us existed, everything else was forgotten. My need to touch her everywhere causing slow trembles as she tightened her grip on my shoulders. From a far away place I heard her cries and started to unravel. Her trembling reverberated through me even as my body hardened like granite. The constant alertness that followed me everywhere slipped away and my pleasure would not be denied. Slowing myself, allowing my lips to tease her nipples. She moaned impatiently, unleashing a torrent of emotions beyond any I'd experienced before, shattering my senses and taking away the last ounce of my control.

A game of combat began, playing out on a soft and seductive battlefield, but as brutal as any war that was ever fought. This battle, however, was being waged with the magic of touch, the exploring tongue and a sword so powerful and precise it extracted her breath while leaving her body supremely alive, trembling for more of the sword's exquisite touch.

Again, tender touches aroused more insistent cries from her as she dug her nails into my arms. I would not give her release but increased her torment. My hands touched and my mouth sucked at the ready nipple. Summoning every shred of mental strength, I gently touched the entrance to the point of her desire, pushing her pleasure and just as her hopeful cries came, I withdrew, afraid to hurt her. But she began to twist her body trying to find what was being denied her. I needed her to give every ounce of herself: to hold back nothing. Moving with her step-by-step raising the heat in every cell in her body, I pushed harder. Her response to my tongue and hands playing together ignited a blazing fire that leapt between us. We moved together as one, each giving life one more chance. All barriers disappeared, leaving only a lover's desire to give everything. She opened herself and accepted every thrust with wild abandon.

I could not bear being separated from her, so pulled her full length along my body. Settling herself, she leaned in pressing tightly. I wanted to give her more, to prolong her pleasure. Lightly brushing her nipple, I felt her reaction. I again caressed her softly which caused a deeper moan. Slowly I moved lower touching her most intimate body. She moved with a rhythm that took away all my defenses. Without letting her go, I turned over and entered her, burying myself deep, watching intense longing burn in her eyes. My emotions caught fire and burned out of control.

~

Later when she opened her eyes, they stared deep into mine. I saw mysterious emotions reflected back at me. They should have frightened her, instead she snuggled closer as I stroked her shoulders softly.

"What are you thinking?" she asked softly, still nestled in my arms. I felt tense emotions radiating from your body."

"About the path that led us to this moment."

"Destiny, maybe?"

"Not necessarily. It could have been chance or luck or even a decision by someone else that set us on the road to this moment. The only way to know is to go back in time and peel away the layers."

Immediately, fear and uncertainty moved to a corner of the room and huddled together waiting for a chance to reassert themselves. There was no place for them in this conversation. Words of hope and determined pronouncements began to speak.

Measuring every word, I began, "Chance and luck determine destiny. By chance Grandma had to run for her life, leaving a family that held a safe, if lonely place for her. Chance took her to church one Sunday where she encountered the person who led her to Sero. Chance continued to hold her in its grip when I was thrust into her life."

"Chance for her, but not for you." She, too was picking her words carefully, trying to follow the paths of these important steps.

Not wanting to be sidetracked, I needed to clarify Grandma's feelings concerning chances. "The idea that something as tenuous as chance played a significant role in her journey to Sero, never set well with her because she considered chance a gambler's prize. For me, on the other hand, all those incidences turned out to be opportunities."

She snuggled closer. Memories needed to flow freely without any interruptions. Eventually they would reveal their importance. Our conversation bounced around different subjects that always returned us to Billy. *Is she purging herself?*

"To lose myself in Billy's power, I could not do. The boundaries were disappearing. My personal rhythm was starting to move with his. We were at the point when my own power had started to diminish."

Is this a warning for me or is she looking for assurance? Being no stranger to power, I knew its dangerous side. Was she now measuring her power against mine with her body? "The balance of power between a man and woman shifts from time to time if the relationship itself makes room for the highs and lows. I would never seek to exert power over you."

"So you say, but it is a man's nature to chase power and dominate."

She touched my lips with two fingers, cutting off my protests and continued, "That natural desire is often hidden, waiting for the right moment to proclaim itself."

"When would that be?"

"At her weakest moment, when her eyes see only the beautiful, and when his power has already claimed her body. It is at the exact moment she is ready to surrender her own power, which is now hobbled by the dynamics of the physical relationship. The risk has now become the prize she is driven to pursue at all costs."

My immediate response was to pull her closer, sliding my fingers gently over the swell of her breast, our bodies again seeking and clinging, concerned only with the magic of touch. *This power I will not run from.* The relentless assault on her senses brought her, once more, to the brink while denying her the relief she begged for. Speech deserted her as she twisted with longing. "No need to hurry, we have all night," I whispered. "I want you to experience a time you will always cherish."

I calmly brushed her skin from shoulders to the swell of her hips, back and forth as she quieted. But my need to feel more of her took hold as she moaned. The assault began again being guided by the cries coming from deep within her: my lips moved slowly down her body in tune with her rising need for release.

"T.J., please," she moaned.

I held her still, my tongue touching her as light as a feather. When I reached a proud nipple, my mouth closed hard as she began to beg aloud. I could no longer hold my own mounting need. With a powerful stroke I took her completely as my mouth cut off her soft scream.

Taking everything from her, in an instant she belonged to me. I slipped away into a void of pleasure I'd never known. My body gave up every drop as she rose to meet me, thrust for thrust. We rode through the void where nothing else existed, just our ancient needs. For an eternal second my breath stopped, and I was alone as my life flowed into her with a surge that lasted an eternity, carrying all my pent-up tension.

I looked down at her face, my pursuit not over. "Look at me."

When she did, I saw, reflected in her eyes, the acceptance of the raw power I'd just implanted, which was still cascading through her body.

In my arms, she slowly drifted into sleep. Then dawn pushed its way into the room just as I rolled over carrying her with me. No words were spoken, I knew we'd entered a place that required us to move forward or run like a rogue wind blowing out of control. Calming myself, I continued to hold her to my chest.

The intermittent conversations we'd had over the past days, were not over. There was more for each of us to know. "There are times when we're required to question our motives. It's not an easy task, but it must be done." I needed to know if she had regrets. I left her no place to hide. "Did you ever think you took the coward's way out?"

"No."

I heard something different in her tone. *What is it you're hiding?* "You and I met by chance, traveling separate paths that led back to a person who changed our lives forever. Billy is our common thread and I sense you wrestling with other reasons you left him: even a measure of guilt. But as we sort through these interesting circumstances, we must keep doubt and suspicion out of the mix."

"Is it your way to push a person until you get the answer you want?'

"I want to know you, not just what I see, but the person who is locked inside of what you show to the world. Once that door opens, we move forward."

"And you also use the bulldozer method."

Sensing the heightening emotions rising in her I tightened my arms around her, waiting to hear more explanations.

"A man wants to control his environment. A woman, on the other hand, is always seeking to exercise power over herself. Only then can she make peace with those around her, including the power of her man. If she doesn't get a handle on her inner person, the fear that she's in the wrong place will never go away. For her the search will go on, always."

Walls were falling away leaving only naked longings. She had entered the uncompromising zone of risk. There was no way back. I was closing the door, leaving her defenses behind. I intended the self-protection she'd worn as a cloak her entire life should offer no protection. As that mythical man of power she'd created, I pushed on, "I will not let you hide from me."

"Wow," she whispered softly.

I've touched the right button. Squeezing tighter, I felt her quick intake of breath. It eased any concern I was pushing too hard.

"I could see the cost of continuing the relationship with Billy was too high; a price. I wouldn't pay."

"Then it wasn't really a bond meant to hold over time."

"I wasn't thinking about time, only the cost of commitment. I wanted only to hold onto the present. Thinking about a future would require me to go back into the past to revisit pain and hurt."

"When two people are building their relationship, running from imagined negative consequences is not an authentic step on the journey." Power would not let go.

"That is the time for the two people to be bold, to face risk of rejection, not hide in a corner. It is the only way."

As the pace of her breathing increased, I unleashed my most powerful arrow, "What you had with Billy was no more special than an ordinary relationship. Your fear of stepping into the cauldron of emotions which might possibly leave you standing alone was too much of a chance for you to take. At a deep level you knew it. You were looking for him to prove himself, to guarantee the sun would never set on what the two of you had at that moment in time. But life guarantees nothing."

Minutes passed without a response from her. I thought she would not answer. Finally, she spoke, so quietly I barely heard her. "Why would he pursue me?"

She wasn't looking for an answer, but I spoke anyway, "Women hide their true nature, requiring men who love them to chase after it. If he is the one meant for her, he will overtake her because he has to know this hidden part of her. Even to make love to her, he must know whether she is more open to him at morning light or when the sun is gone. If he is wrong for her, he will never find the authentic woman. Another man will take up the hunt."

"To what end: the winning of a prize?"

"No, the winning of a treasure, necessary to complete his own nature."

With the swiftness of the next breath, I took her again entering her with a violent thrust that left her suspended, with no place to run.

20

A soothing cup of coffee kept my company as I sat sifting through the consequences that lay ahead. What I thought to be a door closing has, instead, opened onto new unchartered territory. My life is expanding, but with unexpected challenges.

A lifetime habit of observing people and measuring their responses, told me the protective walls Brenda had erected were falling down around her, leaving her without the protection of her own psyche. That hidden self she held close, even from Billy, was now a feeble shadow. Going forward will be tricky.

When she came into the kitchen, there was a wildness about her. She was without makeup, uncombed hair framing her beautiful face. Even now I longed to run my fingers through the thick stands. She came to stand behind me, putting both hands on my shoulders. Reaching up I gave each a gentle squeeze, with the clear understanding we were in a different place, the next step unknown.

"We've crossed a line and can never return to our beginning. What happens now?"

I wasn't sure she was really looking for an answer or just verbalizing her thoughts. Both of us have experience bumping against boundaries. She learned to move on after Billy. On the other hand, with Kena, I have no need to.

"You're hiding something." she whispered.

"What makes you think I have something to hide?"

"I sense it. Could it be you're having regrets, now that you've made love to Billy's girl? You continue pounding me about my motives with him and I sense you're now examining your own motives in your friendship with him." Her fingers gently rubbed the sides of my neck quickening my pulse. Coming around to sit across from me, she reached out and curled her hands around mine, looking directly into my eyes. "Are you also exploring the reasons you've not taken the next step with your child's mother, just as you're pushing me harder to uncover reasons other than those I've given you for ending my time with Billy?"

Do I really need an answer? Yes, open your mind.

She could not guess the conflicting emotions and thoughts going through my mind at that moment. Before she came into the room, I'd asked myself these same questions. Honest answers have become more complicated. Billy relied on me to find this woman. But, could he foresee the same forces that made her special to him, would also be a magnet for another man, maybe me?

"Kena and I never made plans to alter our relationship. Things are fine as they stand."

"So it was with Billy and me. The idea that additional claims would arise terrified me." She was eloquently picking her words. "Then what are you terrified of?"

"Nothing about the relationship."

"That's a cop-out and you know it. A man who wants the ultimate commitment, demands it. He doesn't let chance take charge of such an important step in his life." She leaned in, "You move forward or walk away." Turning her palms up she simultaneously hunched her shoulders. "I ask you again, what do you fear?"

The question finally hit its mark. Immediately a kaleidoscope of women came to mind, one-by-one their images danced before me. From my mother I learned never to trust my life to any woman, not even Kena or Rita. And with Grandma, until I went away to college, I was not able to rid myself of the fear that if I made one mistake, she'd send me away. Before their faces faded, another picture came into focus, one who shows up too many times uninvited: the image of that long-ago woman, naked and white, smooth so like marble, staring straight at me. She meant danger. Standing and moving to the window, I needed a moment to tamp down the image.

"You've slipped away from me, but my question will not go away. Only when you confront the truth, will your fear of trust lose its power."

You are right. She cleverly mixed my past with the present, but I chose to speak on a safer subject: the early days with Billy. "Lately I've come to accept that important memories of my friendship with Billy may have been more myth than reality. Our friendship was born in the loneliness of two young boys who felt bereft of the love of their families. Billy's mother appeared incapable of offering maternal interaction with her children and my mother hid herself from me. I could not have, at any time if my life depended on it, locate her whereabouts on a map. As children we brought to the relationship what we needed and took from it expectations from those needs: time together and a trusted reliance only on each other. You, on the other hand, did not have the time with him for myth to take hold. The two of you existed in the moment, in real time."

Our companionable silence was broken as I turned, ready for whatever she had to say. "I feel there is something more you want to say. Tell me."

"You're everything Billy described. I see why he envied you."

So, discussion of our new situation is temporarily on hold.

"What are you referring to?"

"He talked so much about you and your grandmother, I came to know you were special to him. And he did envy you. We were talking once, and I sensed a tone I hadn't heard before. He believed if he'd paid more attention to how you and your grandmother worked together, he could have had the life you have. And he was sure being black helped you."

"You're kidding?"

"No. I pushed him to explain how he arrived at that conclusion. He responded there was no way out of his hometown without special help. So I suggested, both of you had the same opportunity to leave after high school. But he thought your teachers had special programs for you that his teachers did not offer him"

"Billy had everything he needed to take the road out of Sero: his race, youth and the natural smarts that charmed everyone he encountered. His teachers could have helped him escape his uninspiring environment. But I can't know what happened in his high school, because not one time did I ever enter those doors. We went to different schools. He was right about my teachers. I did get special help from them. They knew I'd have to leave Sero. They helped me find the college I attended, fill out the application for admission and scholarships. Billy was capable, I often saw his report card. He had the grades and I'm sure his teachers encouraged him."

"In addition, you had Grandma."

A warm feeling passed through me. "True, it was her intention to see me out of Sero. She never let up. She understood my life would unfold on a different stage beyond the limiting confines of our little town."

"As you went off to college and began moving forward in your life, you escaped the compartment Billy had placed you, his best friend. In the Sero part of your relationship it didn't matter that you were black. However, when you escaped Sero, leaving him behind, your blackness kicked in. All that you'd been to each other became conflicted. He'd never envisioned you outside that Sero compartment, so there was no frame of reference for him. Shamefully he began to believe you possessed something he should have, a chance: the same chance you were given because of your race."

"I can't accept your explanation, its nonsense."

"Its not my explanation, Billy figured it out."

Her words forced me to recall memories of the two or three weeks I was home during summer breaks from college. We still hung out together, but he was more interested in my life on campus. We rarely talked about what was going on with him while I was away. I had no idea what his life was like during my college years." While these unthinkable words were being thrown at me, my mind sought safety in blankness as her assault continued.

"Whether you're prepared to accept it or not, race finally entered the forever brotherhood between you and Billy, even though you'd decided to be colorblind in this so-called brotherhood. It never works."

Grandma knew. She knew one day I would have to confront the big nut in our friendship. "There was no reason for my racial identity to be significant in Sero: that it shows up long after leaving home, doesn't mean it changes the trust and support we had in each other." My protestations did nothing to stop the creeping doubts.

For the remainder of the day we never returned to the subject. She'd opened the race issue and I needed to process it, unfiltered. We spent the day together. Even with the nagging questions she'd put to me, our time together was pleasant and unhurried and again we passed the night in each other's arms. While Brenda slept in blissful oblivion, I lay awake staring into the darkness trying to clear my head. My thoughts, however, could not escape our morning discussion in the kitchen and her pointed questions that tormented me even during the flight home.

I was forced to sit with the uninvited thoughts and more questions I knew must be dealt with before I'd have a little of the peace I craved. Shutting out the chatter around me and discouraging friendly conversation from my seat mate, I reclined the seat and closed my eyes. The women, as I refer to them, came rolling back. I resented being hostage to each one of them. *Why do I need to justify my decisions to someone so new in my life?* Her importance to me had come unexpectedly and posed another conflict for me. The idea that she'd become a force I couldn't ignore was an annoyance.

Although neither of us spoke the obvious, we knew I'd become a member of the family. I understood it came with certain assumptions. As with any family we are now interdependent, and I've taken on a measure of responsibility for another child. Bill was the first to solidify this new dynamic between the three of us. I'd become Uncle T.J.

His father had time to tell me of their existence, plenty of time, but he chose not to. If he'd spoken of them our discussions might have placed doubts, even crushed his hopes that his life had relevance. By not telling me, he forced me into their lives, to assume the responsibility of making sure they knew every step of his journey. He locked me into a position I couldn't refuse. He won this game after all. Checkmate.

21

During Bill's second visit with Ms. Cady, it was apparent she'd prepared for him. We'd arrived only a short time when she handed him a neatly wrapped package. "Here are some things that belonged to your dad."

"Thank you." He stared at it before slowly removing the wrapping paper. Then he ran his fingers over each one of the books.

"Tell me about them the next time you come."

He hurriedly put them in the car and ran back to the other children. As he played with his cousins, Ms. Cady and I bantered back and forth. She returned to questions about Brenda, trying to get more information about her without asking directly. "What's she like?"

"She's smart, a super mom and a beautiful woman."

"You know quite a bit about her."

"It isn't hard to get to know a person who is open to sharing information about someone both of us cared for. And Billy meant for me to know her."

"Who else did you say lives with them?"

"No one. His mother is single, and his other grandmother has passed away. I don't know much about others. She's from a small family." I decided to raise the temperature a notch. Leaning against the car in a nonthreatening manner,

I needed to speak for Billy. "So, it's important for him to connect to and establish a relationship with this side of his family. Don't you think so?"

"Family never meant much to his father. In his mind, only blood connected us."

"That same blood connects Bill to you and those kids out back. He's your grandson Ms. Cady no matter what went before him between his father and this family."

She seemed to gather herself, tightening her lips, then let the arrows fly, "Are you stepping into Billy's role with him and his mamma?"

"Where Bill is concerned, I'm only doing what Billy would want me to do."

"If you say so, then it must be true, but you still must answer to yourself, whether you accept the place of father and whatever else Billy had in mind."

You must have read my mind.

She had more arrows to sling. Out of nowhere, she pronounced, "When you left Sero, Billy expected you to find a place for him."

"I went to a black school." No further explanation needed, as I was still working through this zinger since Brenda brought it up.

For the remainder of our visit, she had no more questions about Brenda. The visit was no longer than the previous one. Bill was doing what they hoped Billy would do, acknowledge them. This time he gave his grandmother a hug before we drove away. Surprising to me she gave back an enthusiastic embrace, even giving him a kiss on the cheek.

Two weeks later I carried him out to California. Deon understood the circumstances; I wanted him to meet my best friend's son. Immediately, he opened himself to the connection. "Then we can be best friends."

"I think you can." I was surprised by the ease with which he was prepared to accept an unknown child into his life: a child who was becoming an important part of my life.

Bill never closed his eyes during the entire trip. His questions about California were endless. "Does Deon live near the beach? Is the water warm? Will I see whales from the beach?"

As children often do, they met as old pals with no existing barriers. Immediately they began sharing school stories, games, names of friends, likes and unpleasant things that affect boys their age. At the end of our stay they made me promise another get-together soon. Bill extended an invitation for Deon to visit his home.

The contentment I feel with their budding friendship, eases, slightly the edge of my hurt and anger toward Billy. I still long for an explanation that will allow me to hold him blameless for embedding Greg into my life with the power to destroy me, but cannot find one. Instead, I return again and again to our boyhood days and the measure of protection he provided me back in Sero. Then I began to feel a perverse sense of sorrow for him. He could not protect himself from the uncertainties that life brings to everyone. He was born with a clear path to a future paved with all the expectations accompanying his male whiteness. But it was stymied by detached parents and ancient expectations for his people that never reached Sero, and a system that gave him only one nugget, his race. For him, though, it did not shine like gold, instead it turned out to be just a dull scrap of metal.

"Was Greg the race card he finally needed to play?" I hadn't heard Grandma's voice in awhile, but she would not rest. *One for you Grandma. Maybe.*

Whether I'd ever be able to sort through this conflict, was not a sure thing. I was trying as hard as I could to reject Brenda's explanation of how race played into our friendship. Shamefully, each time I try, I feel I need him to help me work through the dilemma. Until Greg, I refused to even consider race had any place in our acceptance of each other. Our friendship flourished in a bubble, undisturbed by the realities around us. Is it really true that only after I left Sero, he found it necessary to grab hold of the racial myths that define our places in the world?

Picking my way through the raging conflict, I avoid any line of thought that leads me to conclude so much of my life is fake. But the questions will not go away. Could it be Billy was playing a game our entire lives and I was his pawn? He sure was smart enough. Even so, brothers sometimes play tricks on each other. To accept Brenda's accusations that we didn't have the brotherhood I claim, would confirm a false reality. I'd then have to accept, even to the end of his life, I took what I needed, while ignoring his need to trust me with the secret knowledge of the woman he loved, and the son they share.

22

Staring into the darkness looking for answers, but finding none, I switched my thoughts to Brenda. Is she now having doubts about her decision to walk away from Billy? Where do I fit into her life? Where does she fit into mine? Am I attracted to her because she once belonged to Billy? If the answer is yes, the next question has to be, why? Just as he wanted to live parts of my life, most of all, finding a path out of Sero: did I covet his devil-may-care attitude, fearlessness and dominant behavior, and now his woman?

At the crack of dawn, we again sat across from each other, neither having slept soundly. A smile came before she began to speak. "I see the storm that kept you awake last night is still raging. I felt you leave the bed early. So, we have more to discuss about Billy."

"I need answers, but have only questions. Number one is, why did he keep you a secret?"

"You said he told you there was a special girl in his life."

"That was all, no details." *Come on now, remember his description of her hair, and how it excited him?*

"Do you remember your response?" She lowered her voice, but insisted, "Or interest?"

"I never discouraged him from talking about anything or anyone. I traveled hundreds of miles just to continue sharing the story of our lives. He had the opportunity at every visit to tell me."

"Yet you still believe he wanted only to hear all the little details of your life, assuming there was nothing in his life worth talking about?"

"No. He should have felt safe telling me. Usually he established the direction of our conversations. Why would I think he was holding secrets about a woman? For the first time I'm forced to consider whether our special friendship was really no more than a myth I created. Billy represented the intersection of the emotional need of a five-year-old for permanent attachments and the shared joys only another child of tender years can provide. The need for a sure and tested friend has never left me. Now as it turns out when I came into his life, he too, at that early age, was searching for a hero to share his journey."

"You see my point. Our strongest needs sometimes occupy such small emotional space, we tend to ignore their potential to disrupt our lives. Then forever after we become slaves to their tyrannical demands. I know. My own emotional need to protect myself from the same fate my mother suffered, caused me to leave a man who held my heart. If I had stayed with him, just being together may have convinced him he had other opportunities. Self preservation prevailed, and it's the same with you. Your need to overcome loneliness and fear of rejection masked your true relationship with him. Was it really a brotherhood or just your raw emotional neediness?"

I hesitated, seeking the right words. "If I could go back in time, would I understand his struggles and respond differently to his pointed questions about fatherhood and my relationship with Deon? Was he looking for me to provide answers about a pathway that would lead him to a relationship with his own son, even from a prison cell?"

"Maybe, maybe not, but you didn't risk finding the truth, just as you're avoiding it now."

"I'm struggling for clarity." Were the visits, sneakers and chump change I deposited into his prison account just the adult manifestations of the myth of brotherhood? Even though he's gone, I live on as the hero who must accompany Bill on this important part of his journey, connecting him to his dad's unrealized hopes.

Throughout the day I reflected on the questions she'd asked. Billy went to his grave knowing every detail of my life. But there is so much more I should have known about his emotional needs: his feelings toward his family, periods in his adult life when we didn't see each other and the woman he loved. Maybe he wanted to unload these secrets. I didn't pick up on the signals: all the extra questions he pressed on me about my son's mother during those last visits.

~

The night was cool and quiet as she lay in my arms, soft and pliant, fresh from our lovemaking. Even with lingering questions, for a short time, my inner struggle quieted. Then the questions without answers returned. Is it unusual for one brother to keep secrets from the other? Will secrets fracture the relationship? Can it be mended? Who can help mend it now? The adults responsible for us played by society's rules, but there were no rules for a lasting friendship like ours. Only Billy and I saw the possibilities. Grandma tolerated things as they were, while diligently preparing me to move on for opportunities beyond Sero. Billy's family assumed he would naturally, as if by magic, take his place in a white man's world. There was nothing they needed to do beyond waiting for his life to unfold as theirs had. But he, on the other hand, expected, when I left, I would make a way for him to follow. Every time I came home, he thought I'd brought hope for him. I never did, just regaled him with stories of my many new discoveries and triumphs. Was I responsible for his hopes? *He was my brother; I had a responsibility to understand his deepest feelings.*

I also grapple with the issues she'd raised about trust. "Who do you trust to stand with you no matter how steep the climb?"

I felt helpless because I had no simple answer. My own complex issues of trust never left me.

"It wasn't trust that you and Billy shared, just dependence."

"You're wrong. I trusted him with my life."

"Oh no. He continued waiting for you to earn his trust. It never happened. You said, even during the visits, your conversations were mostly about your concerns, not his."

I sat up abruptly, moving slightly away from her, needing to defend myself. "I was there for him, doing everything I could, considering his incarceration."

She leaned into my chest, pressing hard. "Trust is a two-way street. Billy did not trust you enough to even hint at the level to which he'd sunk. If he had, you may have been able to rescue him. It's possible he was hoping for that chance or was afraid you would just walk away from all you'd been to each other."

"Billy was still playing our life-long game, What if…?"

"By constructing a deadly set of circumstances?"

"He knew I'd find the answers."

Even in the dark, I saw her pupils widen. "How is it you can't see that neither Billy's actions nor yours were the behaviors of people who trust each other? Even with me he wasn't sure you'd approve of the relationship or find it below the standards you were living."

"Your interpretation of trust is limited. I understand trust based on a decades-long relationship that even survives death. Billy knew I'd find you." I felt the stiffness in her body crumble. "And that I would do for you everything required of me."

"But," she plowed on. "Examine the other relationships in your life. What do they say about trust?"

Finally, the gut punch.

"When there's trust between people, each values the other and is not afraid to be vulnerable. When you and Billy were boys, the glue that held you together was companionship, not trust. You relied on him as a playmate and later, to be a sounding board for your accomplishments and concerns. Not once did you put any part of yourself into his hands for safekeeping. Don't you think its odd you have no knowledge of what his life was like after you went off to college? Or during the years you were climbing the corporate ladder?"

"We were not structuring a friendship: ours was free-flowing. Where was your trust with him?"

"Remember I told you, from the beginning, I didn't bring commitment for a permanent future to my relationship with Billy. My excitement and passion existed in the moment. Trust wasn't required." After a long silence she threw her strongest punch. "What value do you place on this moment, you and me?"

"We give everything to these moments when time loses its relevance. They're irreplaceable." I wasn't sure this was the answer she expected. I'd asked myself the same question. *No answer.*

23

I should have known I was sliding into an unknown place the first time I pulled up to the house. Each time we meet, I'm drawn deeper into a web of emotions and new facts about myself that don't change my understanding of Billy's actions. Nor do they lessen my longing to explore whatever lies ahead with Brenda. Destiny will have its way. My growing need for her slipped up on me before I saw it coming. Is it her powerful physical attractiveness or the final play between Billy and me? Do I win because she was once his? The alert system that has guided most of my life is failing.

These uncertainties with all the other constant questions are using too much mental time. Rita has commented recently on my being distracted. Kena, so far away, recognized my tone of voice is different, more clipped, she described it. Even my assistant recognizes a change in my day-to-day work habits. I have begun pushing my team to perform at breakneck speed. This is unusual because I've always encouraged them to move forward at the speed each chose, knowing they must move in unison to meet every deadline. Usually, projects are completed in a more collegial spirit. Now they are at each other's throats, snapping like angry teens.

But Brenda, goes with the flow of new circumstances in her life, unencumbered by the boundaries of old relationships and attitudes. *What would it feel like to live with that kind of freedom?*

Billy has been dead for almost a year. I'll never be able to put to rest the final chapter involving Greg, but he owns a permanent place in my memories. His journey is forever entwined with mine. He was my brother and his friendship brought into my life an understanding I had choices, even in Sero. Why then didn't I choose to help him make his way in the world outside of Sero? No matter. I have every right to call him brother. Blood would not have made us closer. I will not let Brenda's questions and suspicions destroy that for me. Yet, every time I think I've come to grips with his duplicity, I'm confronted with another challenge to understanding his dual nature. I need to peel back the layers of a lifetime interacting with him and examine each, one by one.

Ours was a friendship that began innocently, just two boys relying on each other for play and companionship. No ambiguity there. But, hiding in a dark place we couldn't see, were racial currents that never receded in our part of the world. Then after so many years, came the inevitable time when our lives began to diverge. My focus changed when I left for college and began building a career. All these activities were taking place far from Sero. Did Billy really expect me to help him leave? To go where? What was my obligation to him?

The layer ablaze with his treachery seems so out of place. But it is in that layer my anger still sits, alternating between compassion for him and my own deep hurt.

Should I have known that my best friend, my brother, harbored a world view colored by racial tints, even he was unable to recognize? On reflection, though, it was predictable his own riskiness was the downhill slope that led him on a direct path to the prison cell where he was to spend the remainder of his days.

Finally, the new, fresh layer: more questions without answers hide there. How should I think of Brenda? What is her meaning in my life? Does her attachment to Billy even matter? Or am I seeing her through the lens of my lifelong issues with trust?

I may never know the reasons he turned against me: something like sibling rivalry, maybe. It's not important now. Lately, however, his keeping Brenda secret burns more than his treachery. I hope in time that will change. She and Bill, like Billy have taken their places in my life and settled into a corner of my heart. *Will I remain uncle T.J. or become T.J., the mentor, protector? Stepdad? I must have an answer based in truth and certainty before I can move forward.*

AUTHOR'S NOTES

1. In the 21st century, the struggles of black men for respect, relevance and acceptance rage on. All of us who love and care for them understand the daily dilemma they face: give in or fight. The ancient fear of violence against them does not fade, but remains fresh, startling in its continued occurrences. Even so, this fear shelters secret dreams kept alive by the burning embers of hope. As mothers, wives, sisters, daughters and lovers we reference the mark of history in our own sacred struggles to support their efforts. They carry a world of baggage unique to them. Therefore, we must never let someone who does not know the weight of their baggage decide the path of our love and support.
2. Yet, we must not forget many of the same fears and conflicts that burden T.J., mirror those of other men, regardless of race or culture. They struggle emotionally to meet the challenges of the ambiguous roles society has assigned them: shifting family roles, gender expectations, even redefining the definition of success in the 21st century.
3. Remember, within the joys of our relationships, we may experience times of disappointment, frustration,

surprise, even betrayal. Is it then necessary to rip apart the entire bond that holds together each link?

Visit with Roz
www.rozkayinc.com